DR. JEKYLL AND MR. HYDE

To everyone who has sometimes worried about his inner self—with its secret passions, desires, impulses to violence—this story about an eminent doctor turned into a fiendish prowler of the night will come as a shocking revelation. Stevenson probes deeply into the so-called split personality and holds the reader's attention with every pulse-throbbing page. Here is a book much too disturbing to be laid aside lightly.

The Reader's Supplement to this ENRICHED CLASSICS edition appears in the center insert. It has been prepared under the supervision of an editorial committee directed by Harry Shefter, Professor of English, New York University, and author of many books used extensively for the improvement of skills in the language arts. The contributing editors for this edition were Hortense H. Levisohn, formerly Principal of William Howard Taft High School, and Leonard R. N. Ashley, Professor of English, Brooklyn College. Grateful acknowledgment is made to the Picture Collection Division of the New York Public Library, which provided much of the illustrative material.

Titles available in the

ENRICHED CLASSICS SERIES

The Adventures of Tom Sawyer • MARK TWAIN
Anne Frank: The Diary of a Young Girl
Billy Budd • HERMAN MELVILLE
The Bridge of San Luis Rey • THORNTON WILDER
Crime and Punishment • FYODOR DOSTOEVSKY
Dr. Jekyll and Mr. Hyde • ROBERT LOUIS STEVENSON
Don Quixote • MIGUEL DE CERVANTES
Fathers and Sons • IVAN TURGENEV
Gulliver's Travels • JONATHAN SWIFT
Heart of Darkness • JOSEPH CONRAD
Life with Father • CLARENCE DAY
Lost Horizon • JAMES HILTON
Lust for Life • IRVING STONE
The Mayor of Casterbridge • THOMAS HARDY
Oedipus the King • SOPHOCLES
The Red Badge of Courage • STEPHEN CRANE
The Return of the Native • THOMAS HARDY
The Scarlet Letter • NATHANIEL HAWTHORNE
Silas Marner • GEORGE ELIOT
Vanity Fair • WILLIAM MAKEPEACE THACKERAY
War and Peace • LEV TOLSTOY
Wuthering Heights • EMILY BRONTË

Robert Louis Stevenson

Dr. Jekyll
and
Mr. Hyde

WASHINGTON SQUARE PRESS ENRICHED CLASSICS
POCKET BOOKS • NEW YORK

DR. JEKYLL AND MR. HYDE

ENRICHED CLASSICS edition published November, 1972

Published by
POCKET BOOKS, a division of Simon & Schuster, Inc.,
630 Fifth Avenue, New York, N.Y.

L

WASHINGTON SQUARE PRESS editions are distributed
in the U.S. by Simon & Schuster, Inc., 630 Fifth Avenue,
New York, N.Y. 10020 and in Canada by Simon & Schuster of Canada, Ltd., Richmond Hill, Ontario, Canada.

ACKNOWLEDGMENTS

"A Distinguished London Home of the Period," photograph by A. F.
Kersting. Reprinted with permission.

"A London Policeman," from *London in the Nineteenth Century* by Sir
Walter Besant, published by A. & C. Black Ltd., London. Reprinted with
permission.

Contents

Dr. Jekyll
and
Mr. Hyde

STORY OF THE DOOR

Mr. Utterson the lawyer was a man of a rugged countenance that was never lighted by a smile; cold, scanty and embarrassed in discourse; backward in sentiment; lean, long, dusty, dreary and yet somehow lovable. At friendly meetings, and when the wine was to his taste, something eminently human beaconed from his eye; something indeed which never found its way into his talk, but which spoke not only in these silent symbols of the after-dinner face, but more often and loudly in the acts of his life. He was austere with himself; drank gin when he was alone, to mortify a taste for vintages; and though he enjoyed the theater, had not crossed the doors of one for twenty years. But he had an approved tolerance for others; sometimes wondering, almost with envy, at the high pressure of spirits involved in their misdeeds; and in any extremity inclined to help rather than to reprove. "I incline to Cain's heresy," he used to say quaintly: "I let my brother go to the devil in his own way." In this character, it was frequently his fortune to be the last reputable acquaintance and the last good influence in the lives of downgoing men. And to such as these, so long as they came about his chambers, he never marked a shade of change in his demeanour.

No doubt the feat was easy to Mr. Utterson; for he was undemonstrative at the best, and even his friendship seemed to be founded in a similar catholicity of good-nature. It is the mark of a modest man to accept his friendly circle ready-made from the hands of opportunity; and that was the lawyer's way. His friends were those of his own blood or those whom he had known the longest; his affections, like ivy, were the growth of time, they implied no aptness in the object. Hence, no doubt, the bond that united him to Mr. Richard Enfield, his distant kinsman, the well-known man about town. It was a nut to crack for many, what these two could see in each other, or what subject they could find in common. It was reported by those who encountered them in their Sunday walks, that they said nothing, looked singularly dull, and would hail with obvious relief the appearance of a friend. For all that, the two men put the greatest store by these excursions, counted them the chief jewel of each week, and not only set aside occasions of pleasure, but even resisted the calls of business, that they might enjoy them uninterrupted.

It chanced on one of these rambles that their way led them down a by-street in a busy quarter of London. The street was small and what is called quiet, but it drove a thriving trade on the week-days. The inhabitants were all doing well, it seemed, and all emulously hoping to do better still, and laying out the surplus of their grains in coquetry; so that the shop fronts stood along that thoroughfare with an air of invitation, like rows of smiling saleswomen. Even on Sunday, when it veiled its more florid charms and lay comparatively empty of passage, the street shone out in contrast to its dingy neighbourhood, like a fire in a forest; and with its freshly painted shutters, well-polished brasses, and general cleanliness and gaiety of note, instantly caught and pleased the eye of the passenger.

Two doors from one corner, on the left hand going east, the line was broken by the entry of a court; and just at that point, a certain sinister block of building thrust forward its gable on the street. It was two storeys high; showed no window, nothing but a door on the lower storey and a blind forehead of discoloured wall on the upper; and bore in every feature, the marks of prolonged and sordid negligence. The door,

3

which was equipped with neither bell nor knocker, was blistered and distained. Tramps slouched into the recess and struck matches on the panels; children kept shop upon the steps; the schoolboy had tried his knife on the mouldings; and for close on a generation, no one had appeared to drive away these random visitors or to repair their ravages.

Mr. Enfield and the lawyer were on the other side of the by-street; but when they came abreast of the entry, the former lifted up his cane and pointed.

"Did you ever remark that door?" he asked; and when his companion had replied in the affirmative, "It is connected in my mind," added he, "with a very odd story."

"Indeed?" said Mr. Utterson, with a slight change of voice, "and what was that?"

"Well, it was this way," returned Mr. Enfield: "I was coming home from some place at the end of the world, about three o'clock of a black winter morning, and my way lay through a part of town where there was literally nothing to be seen but lamps. Street after street, and all the folks asleep—street after street, all lighted up as if for a procession and all as empty as a church— till at last I got into that state of mind when a man listens and listens and begins to long for the sight of a policeman. All at once, I saw two figures: one a little man who was stumping along eastward at a good walk, and the other a girl of maybe eight or ten who was running as hard as she was able down a cross street. Well, sir, the two ran into one another naturally enough at the corner; and then came the horrible part of the thing; for the man trampled calmly over the child's body and left her screaming on the ground. It sounds nothing to hear, but it was hellish to see. It wasn't like a man; it was like some damned Juggernaut. I gave a view halloa, took to my heels, collared my gentleman, and brought him back to where there was already quite a group about the screaming child. He was perfectly cool and made no resistance, but gave me one look, so ugly that it brought out the sweat on me like running. The people who had turned out were the girl's own family; and pretty soon, the doctor, for whom she had been sent, put in his appearance. Well, the child was not much the worse, more frightened, according to the Sawbones; and there you might have supposed would be an end to it. But there was one curious circumstance. I had taken a loathing to my gentleman at first sight. So had the child's family, which was only natural. But the doctor's case was what struck me. He was the usual cut and dry apothecary, of no particular age and colour, with a strong Edinburgh accent, and about as

5

emotional as a bagpipe. Well, sir, he was like the rest of us; every time he looked at my prisoner, I saw that Sawbones turn sick and white with desire to kill him, I knew what was in his mind, just as he knew what was in mine; and killing being out of the question, we did the next best. We told the man we could and would make such a scandal out of this, as should make his name stink from one end of London to the other. If he had any friends or any credit, we undertook that he should lose them. And all the time, as we were pitching it in red hot, we were keeping the women off him as best we could, for they were as wild as harpies. I never saw a circle of such hateful faces; and there was the man in the middle, with a kind of black, sneering coolness—frightened too, I could see that—but carrying it off, sir, really like Satan. 'If you choose to make capital out of this accident,' said he, 'I am naturally helpless. No gentleman but wishes to avoid a scene,' says he. 'Name your figure.' Well, we screwed him up to a hundred pounds for the child's family; he would have clearly liked to stick out; but there was something about the lot of us that meant mischief, and at last he struck. The next thing was to get the money; and where do you think he carried us but to that place with the door?— whipped out a key, went in, and presently came back with the matter of ten pounds in gold and a cheque for the balance on Coutts's, drawn payable to bearer and signed with a name that I can't mention, though it's one of the points of my story, but it was a name at least very well known and often printed. The figure was stiff; but the signature was good for more than that, if it was only genuine. I took the liberty of pointing out to my gentleman that the whole business looked apocryphal, and that a man does not, in real life, walk into a cellar door at four in the morning and come out with another man's cheque for close upon a hundred pounds. But he was quite easy and sneering. 'Set your mind at rest,' says he, 'I will stay with you till the banks open and cash the cheque myself.' So we all set off, the doctor, and the child's father, and our friend and myself, and passed the rest of the night in my chambers; and next day, when we had breakfasted, went in a body to the bank. I gave in the cheque myself, and said I had every reason to believe it was a forgery. Not a bit of it. The cheque was genuine."

"Tut-tut," said Mr. Utterson.

"I see you feel as I do," said Mr. Enfield. "Yes, it's a bad story. For my man was a fellow that nobody could have to do with, a really damnable man; and the person that drew the cheque is the very pink of the proprieties, celebrated too, and (what makes it worse) one of your fellows who do what they call good. Black mail, I suppose; an honest man paying through the nose for some of the capers of his youth. Black Mail House is what I call the place with the door, in consequence. Though even that, you know, is far from explaining all," he added, and with the words fell into a vein of musing.

From this he was recalled by Mr Utterson asking rather suddenly: "And you don't know if the drawer of the cheque lives there?"

"A likely place, isn't it?" returned Mr. Enfield. "But I happen to have noticed his address; he lives in some square or another."

"And you never asked about the—place with the door?" said Mr. Utterson.

"No, sir: I had a delicacy," was the reply. "I feel very strongly about putting questions; it partakes too much of the style of the day of judgment. You start a question, and it's like starting a stone. You sit quietly on the top of a hill; and away the stone goes, starting others; and presently some bland old bird (the last you would have thought of) is knocked on the head in his own back garden and the family have to change their name. No sir, I make it a rule of mine: the more it looks like Queer Street, the less I ask."

"A very good rule, too," said the lawyer.

"But I have studied the place for myself," continued Mr. Enfield. "It seems scarcely a house. There is no other door, and nobody goes in or out of that one but, once in a great while, the gentleman of my adventure. There are three windows looking on the court on the first floor; none below; the windows are always shut but they're clean. And then there is a chimney which is generally smoking; so somebody must live there. And yet it's not so sure; for the buildings are so packed together about the court, that it's hard to say where one ends and another begins."

The pair walked on again for a while in silence; and then "Enfield," said Mr. Utterson, "that's a good rule of yours."

"Yes, I think it is," returned Enfield.

"But for all that," continued the lawyer, "there's one point I want to ask: I want to ask the name of that man who walked over the child."

"Well," said Mr. Enfield, "I can't see what harm it would do. It was a man of the name of Hyde."

"Hm," said Mr. Utterson. "What sort of a man is he to see?"

"He is not easy to describe. There is something wrong with his appearance; something displeasing, something down-right detestable. I never saw a man I so disliked, and yet I scarce know why. He must be deformed somewhere; he gives a strong feeling of deformity, although I couldn't specify the point. He's an extraordinary looking

9

man, and yet I really can name nothing out of the way. No, sir; I can make no hand of it; I can't describe him. And it's not want of memory; for I declare I can see him this moment."

Mr. Utterson again walked some way in silence and obviously under a weight of consideration. "You are sure he used a key?" he inquired at last.

"My dear sir . . ." began Enfield, surprised out of himself.

"Yes, I know," said Utterson; "I know it must seem strange. The fact is, if I do not ask you the name of the other party, it is because I know it already. You see, Richard, your tale has gone home. If you have been inexact in any point, you had better correct it."

"I think you might have warned me," returned the other with a touch of sullenness. "But I have been pedantically exact, as you call it. The fellow had a key; and what's more, he has it still. I saw him use it, not a week ago."

Mr. Utterson sighed deeply but said never a word; and the young man presently resumed. "Here is another lesson to say nothing," said he. "I am ashamed of my long tongue. Let us make a bargain never to refer to this again."

"With all my heart," said the lawyer. "I shake hands on that, Richard."

SEARCH FOR MR. HYDE

That evening Mr. Utterson came home to his
bachelor house in sombre spirits and sat down to
dinner without relish. It was his custom of a
Sunday, when this meal was over, to sit close by
the fire, a volume of some dry divinity on his
reading desk, until the clock of the neighbouring
church rang out the hour of twelve, when he
would go soberly and gratefully to bed. On this
night, however, as soon as the cloth was taken
away, he took up a candle and went into his
business room. There he opened his safe, took from
the most private part of it a document endorsed
on the envelope as Dr. Jekyll's Will, and sat down
with a clouded brow to study its contents. The
will was holograph, for Mr. Utterson, though he
took charge of it now that it was made, had
refused to lend the least assistance in the making
of it; it provided not only that, in case of the
decease of Henry Jekyll, M.D., D.C.L., L.L.D.,

F.R.S., etc., all his possessions were to pass into the hands of his "friend and benefactor Edward Hyde," but that in case of Dr. Jekyll's "disappearance or unexplained absence for any period exceeding three calendar months," the said Edward Hyde should step into the said Henry Jekyll's shoes without further delay and free from any burthen or obligation, beyond the payment of a few small sums to the members of the doctor's household. This document had long been the lawyer's eyesore. It offended him both as a lawyer and as a lover of the sane and customary sides of life, to whom the fanciful was the immodest. And hitherto it was his ignorance of Mr. Hyde that had swelled his indignation; now, by a sudden turn, it was his knowledge. It was already bad enough when the name was but a name of which he could learn no more. It was worse when it began to be clothed upon with detestable attributes; and out of the shifting, insubstantial mists that had so long baffled his eye, there leaped up the sudden, definite presentment of a fiend.

"I thought it was madness," he said, as he replaced the obnoxious paper in the safe, "and now I begin to fear it is disgrace."

With that he blew out his candle, put on a greatcoat and set forth in the direction of Cavendish Square, that citadel of medicine, where his friend, the great Dr. Lanyon, had his house and received his crowding patients. "If anyone knows, it will be Lanyon," he had thought.

The solemn butler knew and welcomed him; he was subjected to no stage of delay, but ushered direct from the door to the dining-room where Dr. Lanyon sat alone over his wine. This was a hearty, healthy, dapper, red-faced gentleman, with a shock of hair prematurely white, and a boisterous and decided manner. At sight of Mr. Utterson, he sprang up from his chair and welcomed him with both hands. The geniality, as was the way of the man, was somewhat theatrical to the eye; but it reposed on genuine feeling. For these two were old friends, old mates both at school and college, both thorough respectors of themselves and of each other, and what does not always follow, men who thoroughly enjoyed each other's company.

After a little rambling talk, the lawyer led up to the subject which so disagreeably preoccupied his mind.

"I suppose, Lanyon," said he, "you and I must be the two oldest friends that Henry Jekyll has?"

"I wish the friends were younger," chuckled Dr. Lanyon. "But I suppose we are. And what of that? I see little of him now."

"Indeed?" said Utterson. "I thought you had a bond of common interest."

"We had," was the reply. "But it is more than ten years since Henry Jekyll became too fanciful for me. He began to go wrong, wrong in mind; and though of course I continue to take an interest in him for old sake's sake, as they say, I see and I have seen devilish little of the man. Such unscientific balderdash," added the doctor, flushing suddenly purple, "would have estranged Damon and Pythias."

This little spirit of temper was somewhat of a relief to Mr. Utterson. "They have only differed on some point of science," he thought; and being a man of no scientific passions (except in the matter of conveyancing), he even added: "It is nothing worse that that!" He gave his friend a few seconds to recover his composure, and then approached the question he had come to put. "Did you ever come across a protégé of his—one Hyde?" he asked.

"Hyde?" repeated Lanyon. "No. Never heard of him. Since my time."

That was the amount of information that the lawyer carried back with him to the great, dark bed on which he tossed to and fro, until the small hours of the morning began to grow large. It was a night of little ease to his toiling mind, toiling in mere darkness and besieged by questions.

Six o'clock struck on the bells of the church that was so conveniently near to Mr. Utterson's dwelling, and still he was digging at the problem. Hitherto it had touched him on the intellectual side alone; but now his imagination also was engaged, or rather enslaved; and as he lay and tossed in the gross darkness of the night and the curtained room, Mr. Enfield's tale went by before his mind in a scroll of lighted pictures. He would be aware of the great field of lamps of a nocturnal city; then of the figure of a man walking swiftly; then of a child running from the doctor's; and then these met, and that human Juggernaut trod the child down and passed on regardless of her screams. Or else he would see a room in a rich house, where his friend lay asleep, dreaming and smiling at his dreams; and then the door of that room would be opened, the curtains of the bed plucked apart, the sleeper recalled, and lo! there would stand by his side a figure to whom power was given, and even at that dead hour, he must rise and do its bidding. The figure in these two phases haunted the lawyer all night; and if at any time he dozed over, it was but to see it glide more stealthily through sleeping houses, or move the more swiftly and still the more swiftly, even to dizziness, through wider labyrinths of lamp-lighted city, and at every street corner crush a child and leave her screaming. And still the

figure had no face by which he might know it;
even in his dreams, it had no face, or one that
baffled him and melted before his eyes; and thus
it was that there sprang up and grew apace in the
lawyer's mind a singularly strong, almost an
inordinate, curiosity to behold the features of the
real Mr. Hyde. If he could but once set eyes on
him, he thought the mystery would lighten and
perhaps roll altogether away, as was the habit of
mysterious things when well examined. He might
see a reason for his friend's strange preference or
bondage (call it which you please) and even for
the startling clause of the will. At least it would
be a face worth seeing: the face of a man who
was without bowels of mercy: a face which had
but to show itself to raise up, in the mind of the
unimpressionable Enfield, a spirit of enduring
hatred.

From that time forward, Mr. Utterson began
to haunt the door in the by-street of shops. In the
morning before office hours, at noon when
business was plenty, and time scarce, at night
under the face of the fogged city moon, by all
lights and at all hours of solitude or concourse,
the lawyer was to be found on his chosen post.

"If he be Mr. Hyde," he had thought, "I shall
be Mr. Seek."

And at last his patience was rewarded. It was a
fine dry night; frost in the air; the streets as clean

as a ballroom floor; the lamps, unshaken by any wind, drawing a regular pattern of light and shadow. By ten o'clock, when the shops were closed, the by-street was very solitary and, in spite of the low growl of London from all round, very silent. Small sounds carried far; domestic sounds out of the houses were clearly audible on either side of the roadway; and the rumour of the approach of any passenger preceded him by a long time. Mr. Utterson had been some minutes at his post, when he was aware of an odd, light footstep drawing near. In the course of his nightly patrols, he had long grown accustomed to the quaint effect with which the footfalls of a single person, while he is still a great way off, suddenly spring out distinct from the vast hum and clatter of the city. Yet his attention had never before been so sharply and decisively arrested; and it was with a strong, superstitious prevision of success that he withdrew into the entry of the court.

The steps drew swiftly nearer, and swelled out suddenly louder as they turned the end of the street. The lawyer, looking forth from the entry, could soon see what manner of man he had to deal with. He was small and very plainly dressed, and the look of him, even at that distance, went somehow strongly against the watcher's inclination. But he made straight for the door, crossing

17

the roadway to save time; and as he came, he drew a key from his pocket like one approaching home.

Mr. Utterson stepped out and touched him on the shoulder as he passed. "Mr. Hyde, I think?"

Mr. Hyde shrank back with a hissing intake of the breath. But his fear was only momentary; and though he did not look the lawyer in the face, he answered coolly enough: "That is my name. What do you want?"

"I see you are going in," returned the lawyer. "I am an old friend of Dr. Jekyll's—Mr. Utterson of Gaunt Street—you must have heard of my name; and meeting you so conveniently, I thought you might admit me."

"You will not find Dr. Jekyll; he is from home," replied Mr. Hyde, blowing in the key. And then suddenly, but without looking up, "How did you know me?" he asked.

"On your side," said Mr. Utterson, "will you do me a favour?"

"With pleasure," replied the other. "What shall it be?"

"Will you let me see your face?" asked the lawyer.

Mr. Hyde appeared to hesitate, and then, as if upon some sudden reflection, fronted about with an air of defiance; and the pair stared at each other pretty fixedly for a few seconds. "Now I shall know you again," said Mr. Utterson. "It may be useful."

"Yes," returned Mr. Hyde, "it is as well we have met; and *à propos*, you should have my address." And he gave a number of a street in Soho.

"Good God!" thought Mr. Utterson, "can he, too, have been thinking of the will?" But he kept his feelings to himself and only grunted in acknowledgment of the address.

"And now," said the other, "how did you know me?"

"By description," was the reply.

"Whose description?"

"We have common friends," said Mr. Utterson.

"Common friends?" echoed Mr. Hyde, a little hoarsely. "Who are they?"

"Jekyll, for instance," said the lawyer.

"He never told you," cried Mr. Hyde, with a flush of anger. "I did not think you would have lied."

"Come," said Mr. Utterson, "that is not fitting language."

The other snarled aloud into a savage laugh; and the next moment with extraordinary quickness, he had unlocked the door and disappeared into the house.

The lawyer stood awhile when Mr. Hyde had left him, the picture of disquietude. Then he began slowly to mount the street, pausing every step or two and putting his hand to his brow like a man in mental perplexity. The problem he was thus debating as he walked, was one of a class that is rarely solved. Mr. Hyde was pale and dwarfish, he gave an impression of deformity without any nameable malformation, he had a displeasing smile, he had borne himself to the lawyer with a sort of murderous mixture of timidity and boldness, and he spoke with a husky, whispering and somewhat broken voice; all these were points against him, but not all of these together could explain the hitherto unknown disgust, loathing and fear with which Mr. Utterson regarded him. "There must be something else," said the perplexed gentleman. "There *is* something more, if I could find a name for it. God bless me, the man seems hardly human! Something troglodytic, shall we say? or can it be the old story of Dr. Fell? or is it the mere radiance of a foul soul that thus transpires through, and transfigures, its clay continent? The last I think; for, O my poor old Harry Jekyll, if ever I read Satan's signature upon a face, it is on that of your new friend."

Round the corner from the by-street, there was a square of ancient, handsome houses, now for the most part decayed from their high estate and let in flats and chambers to all sorts and conditions of men; map-engravers, architects, shady lawyers and the agents of obscure enterprises. One house, however, second from the corner, was still occupied entire; and at the door of this, which wore a great air of wealth and comfort, though it was now plunged in darkness except for the fanlight, Mr. Utterson stopped and knocked. A well-dressed, elderly servant opened the door.

"Is Dr. Jekyll at home, Poole?" asked the lawyer.

"I will see, Mr. Utterson," said Poole, admitting the visitor, as he spoke, into a large, low-roofed, comfortable hall, paved with flags, warmed (after the fashion of a country house) by a bright, open fire, and furnished with costly cabinets of oak. "Will you wait here by the fire, sir? or shall I give you a light in the dining-room?"

"Here, thank you," said the lawyer, and he drew near and leaned on the tall fender. This hall, in which he was now left alone, was a pet fancy of his friend the doctor's; and Utterson himself was wont to speak of it as the pleasantest room in London. But tonight there was a shudder in his blood; the face of Hyde sat heavy on his memory; he felt (what was rare with him) a nausea and distaste of life; and in the gloom of his spirits, he seemed to read a menace in the flickering of the firelight on the polished cabinets and the uneasy starting of the shadow on the roof. He was ashamed of his relief, when Poole presently returned to announce that Dr. Jekyll was gone out.

"I saw Mr. Hyde go in by the old dissecting-room door, Poole," he said. "Is that right, when Dr. Jekyll is from home?"

"Quite right, Mr. Utterson, sir," replied the servant. "Mr. Hyde has a key."

"Your master seems to repose a great deal of trust in that young man, Poole," resumed the other musingly.

"Yes, sir, he does indeed," said Poole. "We have all orders to obey him."

"I do not think I ever met Mr. Hyde?" asked Utterson.

"O, dear no, sir. He never *dines* here," replied the butler. "Indeed we see very little of him on this side of the house; he mostly comes and goes by the laboratory."

"Well, good-night, Poole."

"Good-night, Mr. Utterson."

And the lawyer set out homeward with a very heavy heart. "Poor Harry Jekyll," he thought, "my mind misgives me he is in deep waters! He was wild when he was young; a long while ago to be sure; but in the law of God, there is no statute of limitations. Ay, it must be that; the ghost of some old sin, the cancer of some concealed disgrace: punishment coming, *pede claudo,* years after memory has forgotten and self-love condoned the fault." And the lawyer, scared by the thought, brooded awhile on his own past, groping in all the corners of memory, lest by chance some Jack-in-the-Box of an old iniquity should leap to light there. His past was fairly blameless; few men could read the rolls of their life with less apprehension; yet he was humbled to the dust by the many ill things he had done, and raised up again into a sober and fearful gratitude by the many he had come so near to doing, yet avoided. And then by a return on his former subject, he conceived a spark of hope. "This Master Hyde, if he were studied," thought he, "must have secrets of his own; black secrets, by the look of him; secrets compared to which poor Jekyll's worst would be like sunshine. Things cannot continue as they are. It turns me cold to think of this creature stealing like a thief to Harry's bedside; poor Harry, what a wakening! And the danger of it; for if this Hyde suspects the existence of the will, he may grow impatient to inherit. Ay, I must put my shoulders to the wheel—if Jekyll will but let me," he added, "if Jekyll will only let me." For once more he saw before his mind's eye, as clear as transparency, the strange clauses of the will.

DR. JEKYLL
WAS QUITE AT EASE

A FORTNIGHT later, by excellent good fortune, the doctor gave one of his pleasant dinners to some five or six old cronies, all intelligent, reputable men and all judges of good wine; and Mr. Utterson so contrived that he remained behind after the others had departed. This was no new arrangement, but a thing that had befallen many scores of times. Where Utterson was liked, he was liked well. Hosts loved to detain the dry lawyer, when the light-hearted and loose-tongued had already their foot on the threshold; they liked to sit awhile in his unobtrusive company, practising for solitude, sobering their minds in the man's rich silence after the expense and strain of gaiety. To this rule, Dr. Jekyll was no exception; and as he now sat on the opposite side of the fire—a large, well-made, smooth-faced man of fifty, with something of a slyish cast perhaps, but every mark of capacity and kindness—you could see by his looks that he cherished for Mr. Utterson a sincere and warm affection.

"I have been wanting to speak to you, Jekyll," began the latter. "You know that will of yours?"

A close observer might have gathered that the topic was distasteful; but the doctor carried it off gaily. "My poor Utterson," said he, "you are unfortunate in such a client. I never saw a man so distressed as you were by my will; unless it were that hide-bound pedant, Lanyon, at what he called my scientific heresies. O, I know he's a good fellow—you needn't frown—an excellent fellow, and I always mean to see more of him; but a hide-bound pedant for all that; an ignorant, blatant pedant. I was never more disappointed in any man than Lanyon."

"You know I never approved of it," pursued Utterson, ruthlessly disregarding the fresh topic.

"My will? Yes, certainly, I know that," said the doctor, a trifle sharply. "You have told me so."

"Well, I tell you so again," continued the lawyer. "I have been learning something of young Hyde."

The large handsome face of Dr. Jekyll grew pale to the very lips, and there came a blackness about his eyes. "I do not care to hear more," said he. "This is a matter I thought we had agreed to drop."

"What I heard was abominable," said Utterson.

"It can make no change. You do not understand my position," returned the doctor, with a certain incoherency of manner. "I am painfully situated, Utterson; my position is a very strange—a very strange one. It is one of those affairs that cannot be mended by talking."

"Jekyll," said Utterson, "you know me: I am a man to be trusted. Make a clean breast of this in confidence; and I make no doubt I can get you out of it."

"My good Utterson," said the doctor, "this is very good of you, this is downright good of you, and I cannot find words to thank you in. I believe you fully; I would trust you before any man alive, ay, before myself, if I could make the choice; but indeed it isn't what you fancy; it is not as bad as that; and just to put your heart at rest, I will tell you one thing: the moment I choose, I can be rid of Mr. Hyde. I give you my hand upon that; and I thank you again and again; and I will just add one little word, Utterson, that I'm sure you'll take in good part: this is a private matter, and I beg of you to let it sleep."

Utterson reflected a little, looking in the fire.

"I have no doubt you are perfectly right," he said at last, getting to his feet.

"Well, but since we have touched upon this business, and for the last time I hope," continued the doctor, "there is one point I should like you to understand. I have really a very great interest in poor Hyde. I know you have seen him; he told me so; and I fear he was rude. But I do sincerely take a great, a very great interest in that young man; and if I am taken away, Utterson, I wish you to promise me that you will bear with him and get his rights for him. I think you would, if you knew all; and it would be a weight off my mind if you would promise."

"I can't pretend that I shall ever like him," said the lawyer.

"I don't ask that," pleaded Jekyll, laying his hand upon the other's arm; "I only ask for justice; I only ask you to help him for my sake, when I am no longer here."

Utterson heaved an irrepressible sigh. "Well," said he, "I promise."

THE CAREW
MURDER CASE

Nearly a year later, in the month of October, 18—, London was startled by a crime of singular ferocity and rendered all the more notable by the high position of the victim. The details were few and startling. A maid servant living alone in a house not far from the river, had gone upstairs to bed about eleven. Although a fog rolled over the city in the small hours, the early part of the night was cloudless, and the lane, which the maid's window overlooked, was brilliantly lit by the full moon. It seems she was romantically given, for she sat down upon her box, which stood immediately under the window, and fell into a dream of musing. Never (she used to say, with streaming tears, when she narrated that experience), never had she felt more at peace with all men or thought more kindly of the world. And as she so sat she became aware of an aged beautiful gentleman with white hair, drawing

near along the lane; and advancing to meet him,
another and very small gentleman, to whom at
first she paid less attention. When they had come
within speech (which was just under the maid's
eyes) the older man bowed and accosted the
other with a very pretty manner of politeness. It
did not seem as if the subject of his address were
of great importance; indeed, from his pointing, it
sometimes appeared as if he were only inquiring
his way; but the moon shone on his face as he
spoke, and the girl was pleased to watch it, it
seemed to breathe such an innocent and old-
world kindness of disposition, yet with something
high too, as of a well-founded self-content.
Presently her eye wandered to the other, and she
was surprised to recognise in him a certain Mr.
Hyde, who had once visited her master and for
whom she had conceived a dislike. He had in his
hand a heavy cane, with which he was trifling;
but he answered never a word, and seemed to
listen with an ill-contained impatience. And then
all of a sudden he broke out in a great flame of
anger, stamping with his foot, brandishing the
cane, and carrying on (as the maid described it)
like a madman. The old gentleman took a step
back, with the air of one very much surprised and
a trifle hurt; and at that Mr. Hyde broke out of all
bounds and clubbed him to the earth. And next
moment, with ape-like fury, he was trampling

his victim under foot and hailing down a storm of blows, under which the bones were audibly shattered and the body jumped upon the roadway. At the horror of these sights and sounds, the maid fainted.

It was two o'clock when she came to herself and called for the police. The murderer was gone long ago; but there lay his victim in the middle of the lane, incredibly mangled. The stick with which the deed had been done, although it was of some rare and very tough and heavy wood, had broken in the middle under the stress of this insensate cruelty; and one splintered half had rolled in the neighbouring gutter—the other, without doubt, had been carried away by the murderer. A purse and gold watch were found upon the victim: but no cards or papers, except a sealed and stamped envelope, which he had been probably carrying to the post, and which bore the name and address of Mr. Utterson.

This was brought to the lawyer the next morning, before he was out of bed; and he had no sooner seen it, and been told the circumstances, than he shot out a solemn lip. "I shall say nothing till I have seen the body," said he; "this may be very serious. Have the kindness to wait while I dress." And with the same grave countenance he hurried through his breakfast and drove to the police station, whither the body had been carried.

As soon as he came into the cell, he nodded.

"Yes," said he, "I recognise him. I am sorry to say that this is Sir Danvers Carew."

"Good God, sir," exclaimed the officer, "is it possible?" And the next moment his eye lighted up with professional ambition. "This will make a deal of noise," he said. "And perhaps you can help us to the man." And he briefly narrated what the maid had seen, and showed the broken stick.

Mr. Utterson had already quailed at the name of Hyde; but when the stick was laid before him, he could doubt no longer; broken and battered as it was, he recognized it for one that he had himself presented many years before to Henry Jekyll.

"Is this Mr. Hyde a person of small stature?" he inquired.

"Particularly small and particularly wicked-looking, is what the maid calls him," said the officer.

Mr. Utterson reflected; and then, raising his head, "If you will come with me in my cab," he said, "I think I can take you to his house."

It was by this time about nine in the morning, and the first fog of the season. A great chocolate-coloured pall lowered over heaven, but the wind was continually charging and routing these embattled vapours; so that as the cab crawled from street to street, Mr. Utterson beheld a marvelous number of degrees and hues of twilight; for here it would be dark like the back-end of evening; and there would be a glow of a rich, lurid brown, like the light of some strange conflagration; and here, for a moment, the fog would be quite broken up, and a haggard shaft of daylight would glance in between the swirling wreaths. The dismal quarter of Soho seen under these changing glimpses, with its muddy ways, and slatternly passengers, and its lamps, which had never been extinguished or had been kindled afresh to combat this mournful reinvasion of darkness, seemed, in the lawyer's eyes, like a district of some city in a nightmare. The thoughts of his mind, besides, were of the gloomiest dye; and when he glanced at the companion of his drive, he was conscious of some touch of that terror of the law and the law's officers, which may at times assail the most honest.

As the cab drew up before the address indicated, the fog lifted a little and showed him a dingy street, a gin palace, a low French eating house, a shop for the retail of penny numbers and twopenny salads, many ragged children huddled in the doorways, and many women of many different nationalities passing out, key in hand, to have a morning glass; and the next moment the fog settled down again upon that part, as brown as umber, and cut him off from his blackguardly surroundings. This was the home of Henry Jekyll's favourite; of a man who was heir to a quarter of a million sterling.

An ivory-faced and silvery-haired old woman opened the door. She had an evil face, smoothed by hypocrisy: but her manners were excellent. Yes, she said, this was Mr. Hyde's, but he was not at home; he had been in that night very late, but he had gone away again in less than an hour; there was nothing strange in that; his habits were very irregular, and he was often absent; for instance, it was nearly two months since she had seen him till yesterday.

"Very well, then, we wish to see his rooms," said the lawyer; and when the woman began to declare it was impossible, "I had better tell you who this person is," he added. "This is Inspector Newcomen of Scotland Yard."

A flash of odious joy appeared upon the woman's face. "Ah!" said she, "he is in trouble! What has he done?"

Mr. Utterson and the inspector exchanged glances. "He don't seem a very popular character," observed the latter. "And now, my good woman, just let me and this gentleman have a look about us."

In the whole extent of the house, which but for the old woman remained otherwise empty, Mr. Hyde had only used a couple of rooms; but these were furnished with luxury and good taste. A closet was filled with wine; the plate was of silver, the napery elegant; a good picture hung upon the walls, a gift (as Utterson supposed) from Henry Jekyll, who was much of a connoisseur; and the carpets were of many plies and agreeable in colour. At this moment, however, the rooms bore every mark of having been recently and hurriedly ransacked; clothes lay about the floor, with their pockets inside out; lock-fast drawers stood open; and on the hearth there lay a pile of grey ashes, as though many papers had been burned. From these embers the inspector disinterred the butt end of a green cheque book, which had resisted the action of the fire; the other half of the stick was found behind the door; and as this clinched his suspicions, the officer declared himself delighted. A visit to the bank, where several thousand pounds were found to be lying to the murderer's credit, completed his gratification.

"You may depend upon it, sir," he told Mr. Utterson: "I have him in my hand. He must have lost his head, or he never would have left the stick or, above all, burned the cheque book. Why, money's life to the man. We have nothing to do but wait for him at the bank, and get out the handbills."

This last, however, was not so easy of

accomplishment; for Mr. Hyde had numbered few familiars—even the master of the servant maid had only seen him twice; his family could nowhere be traced; he had never been photographed; and the few who could describe him differed widely, as common observers will. Only on one point were they agreed; and that was the haunting sense of unexpressed deformity with which the fugitive impressed his beholders.

INCIDENT
OF THE LETTER

It was late in the afternoon, when Mr. Utterson found his way to Dr. Jekyll's door, where he was at once admitted by Poole, and carried down by the kitchen offices and across a yard which had once been a garden, to the building which was indifferently known as the laboratory or dissecting rooms. The doctor had bought the house from the heirs of a celebrated surgeon; and his own tastes being rather chemical than anatomical, had changed the destination of the block at the bottom of the garden. It was the first time that the lawyer had been received in that part of his friend's quarters; and he eyed the dingy, windowless structure with curiosity, and gazed round with a distasteful sense of strangeness as he crossed the theatre, once crowded with eager students and now lying gaunt and silent, the tables laden with chemical apparatus, the floor strewn with crates and littered with packing straw, and the light falling dimly through the foggy cupola. At the further end, a flight of stairs mounted to a door covered with red baize; and through this, Mr. Utterson was at last received into the doctor's cabinet. It was a large room fitted round with glass presses, furnished, among other things, with a cheval-glass and a business table, and looking out upon the court by three dusty windows barred with iron. The fire burned in the grate; a lamp was set lighted on the chimney shelf, for even in the houses the fog began to lie thickly; and there, close up to the warmth, sat Dr. Jekyll, looking deathly sick. He did not rise to meet his visitor, but held out a cold hand and bade him welcome in a changed voice.

"And now," said Mr. Utterson, as soon as Poole had left them, "you have heard the news?"

The doctor shuddered. "They were crying it in the square," he said. "I heard them in my dining-room."

"One word," said the lawyer. "Carew was my client, but so are you, and I want to know what I am doing. You have not been mad enough to hide this fellow?"

"Utterson, I swear to God," cried the doctor, "I swear to God I will never set eyes on him again. I bind my honour to you that I am done with him in this world. It is all at an end. And indeed he does not want my help; you do not know him as I do; he is safe, he is quite safe; mark my words, he will never more be heard of."

The lawyer listened gloomily; he did not like his friend's feverish manner. "You seem pretty sure of him," said he; "and for your sake, I hope you may be right. If it came to a trial, your name might appear."

"I am quite sure of him," replied Jekyll; "I have grounds for certainty that I cannot share with anyone. But there is one thing on which you may advise me. I have—I have received a letter; and I am at a loss whether I should show it to the police. I should like to leave it in your hands, Utterson; you would judge wisely, I am sure; I have so great a trust in you."

"You fear, I suppose, that it might lead to his detection?" asked the lawyer.

"No," said the other. "I cannot say that I care what becomes of Hyde; I am quite done with him. I was thinking of my own character, which this hateful business has rather exposed."

Utterson ruminated awhile; he was surprised at his friend's selfishness, and yet relieved by it. "Well," said he, at last, "let me see the letter."

The letter was written in an odd, upright hand and signed "Edward Hyde": and it signified, briefly enough, that the writer's benefactor, Dr. Jekyll, whom he had long so unworthily repaid for a thousand generosities, need labour under no alarm for his safety, as he had means of escape on which he placed a sure dependence. The lawyer liked this letter well enough; it put a better colour on the intimacy than he had looked for; and he blamed himself for some of his past suspicions.

"Have you the envelope?" he asked.

"I burned it," replied Jekyll, "before I thought what I was about. But it bore no postmark. The note was handed in."

"Shall I keep this and sleep upon it?" asked Utterson.

"I wish you to judge for me entirely," was the reply. "I have lost confidence in myself."

"Well, I shall consider," returned the lawyer. "And now one word more: it was Hyde who dictated the terms in your will about that disappearance?"

The doctor seemed seized with a qualm of faintness; he shut his mouth tight and nodded.

"I knew it," said Utterson. "He meant to murder you. You had a fine escape."

"I have had what is far more to the purpose," returned the doctor solemnly: "I have had a lesson—O God, Utterson, what a lesson I have had!" And he covered his face for a moment with his hands.

On his way out, the lawyer stopped and had a

word or two with Poole. "By the bye," said he, "there was a letter handed in to-day: what was the messenger like?" But Poole was positive nothing had come except by post; "and only circulars by that," he added.

This news sent off the visitor with his fears renewed. Plainly the letter had come by the laboratory door; possibly, indeed, it had been written in the cabinet; and if that were so, it must be differently judged, and handled with the more caution. The newsboys, as he went, were crying themselves hoarse along the footways: "Special edition. Shocking murder of an M.P." That was the funeral oration of one friend and client; and he could not help a certain apprehension lest the good name of another should be sucked down in the eddy of the scandal. It was, at least, a ticklish decision that he had to make; and self-reliant as he was by habit, he began to cherish a longing for advice. It was not to be had directly; but perhaps, he thought, it might be fished for.

Presently after, he sat on one side of his own hearth, with Mr. Guest, his head clerk, upon the other, and midway between, at a nicely calculated distance from the fire, a bottle of a particular old wine that had long dwelt unsunned in the foundations of his house. The fog still slept on the wing above the drowned city, where the lamps glimmered like carbuncles; and through the muffle and smother of these fallen clouds, the procession of the town's life was still rolling in through the great arteries with a sound as of a mighty wind. But the room was gay with firelight. In the bottle the acids were long ago resolved; the imperial dye had softened with time, as the colour grows richer in stained windows; and the glow of hot autumn afternoons on hillside vineyards, was ready to be set free and to disperse the fogs of London. Insensibly the lawyer melted. There was no man from whom he kept fewer secrets than Mr. Guest; and he was not always sure that he kept as many as he meant. Guest had often been on business to the doctor's; he knew Poole; he could scarce have failed to hear of Mr. Hyde's familiarity about the house; he might draw conclusions: was it not as well, then, that he should see a letter which put that mystery to rights? and above all since Guest, being a great student and critic of handwriting, would consider the step natural and obliging? The clerk, besides, was a man of counsel; he could scarce read so strange a document without dropping a remark; and by that remark Mr. Utterson might shape his future course.

"This is a sad business about Sir Danvers," he said.

"Yes, sir, indeed. It has elicited a great deal of

public feeling," returned Guest. "The man, of course, was mad,"

"I should like to hear your views on that," replied Utterson. "I have a document here in his handwriting; it is between ourselves, for I scarce know what to do about it; it is an ugly business at the best. But there it is; quite in your way: a murderer's autograph."

Guest's eyes brightened, and he sat down at once and studied it with passion. "No sir," he said: "not mad; but it is an odd hand."

"And by all acounts a very odd writer," added the lawyer.

Just then the servant entered with a note.

"Is that from Dr. Jekyll, sir?" inquired the clerk. "I thought I knew the writing. Anything private, Mr. Utterson?"

"Only an invitation to dinner. Why? Do you want to see it?"

"One moment. I thank you, sir;" and the clerk laid the two sheets of paper alongside and sedulously compared their contents. "Thank you, sir," he said at last, returning both; "it's a very interesting autograph."

There was a pause, during which Mr. Utterson struggled with himself. "Why did you compare them, Guest?" he inquired suddenly.

"Well, sir," returned the clerk, "there's a rather

singular resemblance; the two hands are in many points identical: only differently sloped."

"Rather quaint," said Utterson.

"It is, as you say, rather quaint," returned Guest.

"I wouldn't speak of this note, you know," said the master.

"No, sir," said the clerk. "I understand."

But no sooner was Mr. Utterson alone that night, than he locked the note into his safe, where it reposed from that time forward. "What!" he thought. "Henry Jekyll forge for a murderer!" and his blood ran cold in his veins.

REMARKABLE INCIDENT
OF DR. LANYON

TIME ran on; thousands of pounds were offered in reward, for the death of Sir Danvers was resented as a public injury; but Mr. Hyde had disappeared out of the ken of the police as though he had never existed. Much of his past was unearthed, indeed, and all disreputable: tales came out of the man's cruelty, at once so callous and violent; of his vile life, of his strange associates, of the hatred that seemed to have surrounded his career; but of his present whereabouts, not a whisper. From the time he had left the house in Soho on the morning of the murder, he was simply blotted out; and gradually, as time drew on, Mr. Utterson began to recover from the hotness of his alarm, and to grow more at quiet with himself. The death of Sir Danvers was, to his way of thinking, more than paid for by the disappearance of Mr. Hyde. Now that that evil influence had been withdrawn, a new life began for Dr. Jekyll. He came out of his seclusion, renewed relations with his friends, became once more their familiar guest and entertainer; and whilst he had always been known for charities, he was now no less distinguished for religion. He was busy, he was much in the open air, he did good; his face seemed to open and brighten, as if with an inward consciousness of service; and for more than two months, the doctor was at peace.

On the 8th of January Utterson had dined at the doctor's with a small party; Lanyon had been there; and the face of the host had looked from one to the other as in the old days when the trio were inseparable friends. On the 12th, and again on the 14th, the door was shut against the lawyer. "The doctor was confined to the house," Poole said, "and saw no one." On the 15th, he tried again, and was again refused; and having now been used for the last two months to see his friend almost daily, he found this return of solitude to weigh upon his spirits. The fifth night he had in Guest to dine with him; and the sixth he betook himself to Dr. Lanyon's.

There at least he was not denied admittance; but when he came in, he was shocked at the change which had taken place in the doctor's appearance. He had his death-warrant written legibly upon his face. The rosy man had grown pale; his flesh had fallen away; he was visibly balder and older; and yet it was not so much these tokens of a swift physical decay that arrested the lawyer's notice, as a look in the eye and quality of manner that seemed to testify to some deep-seated terror of the mind. It was unlikely that the doctor should fear death; and yet that was what Utterson was tempted to suspect. "Yes," he thought; "he is a doctor, he must know his own state and that his days are counted; and the knowledge is more than he can bear." And yet when Utterson remarked on his ill-looks, it was with an air of great firmness that Lanyon declared himself a doomed man,

"I have had a shock," he said, "and I shall never recover. It is a question of weeks. Well, life has been pleasant; I liked it; yes, sir, I used to like it. I sometimes think if we knew all, we should be more glad to get away."

"Jekyll is ill, too," observed Utterson. "Have you seen him?"

But Lanyon's face changed, and he held up a trembling hand. "I wish to see or hear no more of Dr. Jekyll," he said in a loud, unsteady voice. "I am quite done with that person; and I beg that you will spare me any allusion to one whom I regard as dead."

"Tut-tut," said Mr. Utterson; and then after a considerable pause, "Can't I do anything?" he inquired. "We are three very old friends, Lanyon; we shall not live to make others."

"Nothing can be done," returned Lanyon; "ask himself."

"He will not see me," said the lawyer.

"I am not surprised at that," was the reply. "Some day, Utterson, after I am dead, you may perhaps come to learn the right and wrong of this. I cannot tell you. And in the meantime, if you can sit and talk with me of other things, for God's sake, stay and do so; but if you cannot keep clear of this accursed topic, then in God's name, go, for I cannot bear it."

As soon as he got home, Utterson sat down and wrote to Jekyll, complaining of his exclusion from the house, and asking the cause of this unhappy break with Lanyon; and the next day brought him a long answer, often very pathetically worded, and sometimes darkly mysterious in drift. The quarrel with Lanyon was incurable. "I do not blame our old friend," Jekyll wrote, "but I share his view that we must never meet. I mean from henceforth to lead a life of extreme seclusion; you must not be surprised, nor must you doubt my friendship, if my door is often shut even to you. You must suffer me to go my own dark way. I have brought on myself a punishment and a danger that I cannot name. If I am the chief of sinners, I am the chief of sufferers also. I could not think that this earth contained a place for sufferings and terrors so unmanning; and you can do but one thing, Utterson, to lighten this destiny, and that is to respect my silence." Utterson was amazed; the dark influence of Hyde had been withdrawn, the doctor had returned to his old tasks and amities; a week ago, the prospect had smiled with every promise of a cheerful and an honoured age; and now in a moment, friendship, and peace of mind, and the whole tenor of his life were wrecked. So great and unprepared a change pointed to madness; but in view of Lanyon's manner and words, there must lie for it some deeper ground.

A week afterwards Dr. Lanyon took to his bed, and in something less than a fortnight he was dead. The night after the funeral, at which he had been sadly affected, Utterson locked the door of his business room, and sitting there by the light of a melancholy candle, drew out and set before him an envelope addressed by the hand and sealed with the seal of his dead friend. "PRIVATE: for the hands of G. J. Utterson ALONE, and in case of his predecease *to be destroyed unread,*" so it was emphatically superscribed; and the lawyer dreaded to behold the contents. "I have buried one friend to-day," he thought: "what if this should cost me another?" And then he condemned the fear as a disloyalty, and broke the seal. Within there was another enclosure, likewise sealed, and marked upon the cover as "not to be opened till the death or disappearance of Dr. Henry Jekyll." Utterson could not trust his eyes. Yes, it was disappearance; here again, as in the mad will which he had long ago restored to its author, here again were the idea of a disappearance and the name of Henry Jekyll bracketted. But in the will, that idea had sprung from the sinister suggestion of the man Hyde; it was set there with a purpose all too plain and horrible. Written by the hand of Lanyon, what should it mean? A great curiosity came on the trustee, to disregard the prohibition and dive at once to the bottom of these mysteries; but professional honour and faith to his dead friend were stringent obligations; and the packet slept in the inmost corner of his private safe.

It is one thing to mortify curiosity, another to conquer it; and it may be doubted if, from that day forth, Utterson desired the society of his surviving friend with the same eagerness. He thought of him kindly; but his thoughts were disquieted and fearful. He went to call indeed; but he was perhaps relieved to be denied admittance; perhaps, in his heart, he preferred to speak with Poole upon the doorstep and surrounded by the air and sounds of the open city, rather than to be admitted into that house of voluntary bondage, and to sit and speak with its inscrutable recluse. Poole had, indeed, no very pleasant news to communicate. The doctor, it appeared, now more than ever confined himself to the cabinet over the laboratory, where he would sometimes even sleep; he was out of spirits, he had grown very silent, he did not read; it seemed as if he had something on his mind. Utterson became so used to the unvarying character of these reports, that he fell off little by little in the frequency of his visits.

INCIDENT
AT THE WINDOW

IT chanced on Sunday, when Mr. Utterson was on his usual walk with Mr. Enfield, that their way lay once again through the by-street; and that when they came in front of the door, both stopped to gaze on it.

"Well," said Enfield, "that story's at an end at least. We shall never see more of Mr. Hyde."

"I hope not," said Utterson. "Did I ever tell you that I once saw him, and shared your feeling of repulsion?"

"It was impossible to do the one without the other," returned Enfield. "And by the way, what an ass you must have thought me, not to know that this was a back way to Dr. Jekyll's! It was partly your own fault that I found it out, even when I did."

"So you found it out, did you?" said Utterson. "But if that be so, we may step into the court and take a look at the windows. To tell you the truth,

I am uneasy about poor Jekyll; and even outside, I feel as if the presence of a friend might do him good."

The court was very cool and a little damp, and full of premature twilight, although the sky, high up overhead, was still bright with sunset. The middle one of the three windows was half-way open; and sitting close beside it, taking the air with an infinite sadness of mien, like some disconsolate prisoner, Utterson saw Dr. Jekyll.

"What! Jekyll!" he cried. "I trust you are better."

"I am very low, Utterson," replied the doctor drearily, "very low. It will not last long, thank God."

"You stay too much indoors," said the lawyer. "You should be out, whipping up the circulation like Mr. Enfield and me. (This is my cousin—Mr. Enfield—Dr. Jekyll.) Come now; get your hat and take a quick turn with us."

"You are very good," sighed the other. "I should like to very much; but no, no, no, it is quite impossible; I dare not. But indeed, Utterson, I am very glad to see you; this is really a great pleasure; I would ask you and Mr. Enfield up, but the place is really not fit."

"Why, then," said the lawyer, good-naturedly, "the best thing we can do is to stay down here and speak with you from where we are."

"That is just what I was about to venture to propose," returned the doctor with a smile. But the words were hardly uttered, before the smile was struck out of his face and succeeded by an expression of such abject terror and despair, as froze the very blood of the two gentlemen below. They saw it but for a glimpse for the window was instantly thrust down; but that glimpse had been sufficient, and they turned and left the court without a word. In silence, too, they traversed the by-street; and it was not until they had come into a neighbouring thoroughfare, where even upon a Sunday there were still some stirrings of life, that Mr. Utterson at last turned and looked at his companion. They were both pale; and there was an answering horror in their eyes.

"God forgive us, God forgive us," said Mr. Utterson.

But Mr. Enfield only nodded his head very seriously, and walked on once more in silence.

Reader's Supplement

to

DR. JEKYLL AND MR. HYDE

ROBERT LOUIS STEVENSON (1850–1894)

BIOGRAPHICAL BACKGROUND

The son of an engineer who built lighthouses, Robert
Louis Stevenson went to the University of Edinburgh at
the age of seventeen to study engineering and later studied
to be a lawyer (like Utterson in the story), though he
never practiced. As a wild man-about-town at college, he
became familiar with all the low dives of the city, perhaps gaining some insight into the criminal mind (or at
least some "atmosphere") which he could later use in
Dr. Jekyll and Mr. Hyde. At the same time he rebelled
against the dour Calvinist upbringing he had been given,
though it left an obvious stamp on his literary work. All
his life he seemed predisposed to concern himself in his
fiction with oppositions of good and evil, innate depravity,
and other metaphysical questions, all of which he continued to see in terms of moral ambiguities and psychological tensions. His Scottish nurse, who had terrified him
"with the fires of hell," had more influence on him than
she could ever have known.

As a boy, Stevenson steeped himself in Scottish history.
This in time led to his writing *Kidnapped* (1886) and
The Master of Ballantrae (1889), a study in evil which
bears many points of resemblance to *Dr. Jekyll and Mr.
Hyde.* Stevenson's reading also strongly impressed upon
his mind several characters who might well have served
him when he came to write *Dr. Jekyll and Mr. Hyde,*
chief among them Deacon Brodie (hanged in 1788), a
pious and inoffensive man who led a double life, being
also the daring and ruthless head of a gang of thieves and
cutthroats.

In his private life, Stevenson's association with women
much older than himself, including a Mrs. Osbourne (an
American lady whom he followed to California and mar-

ried in 1880, after she had divorced her first husband),
showed an indifference to public opinion. Oddly enough,
this firm and rather frightening woman was able to exer-
cise quite an influence over *Dr. Jekyll and Mr. Hyde,* as is
indicated in the Historical Background. Perhaps in loving
her, in defiance of his strict Presbyterian background,
Stevenson was giving in to that private self, the one that
chafes at the dictates of society and the restrictions of
convention, and was the better able to draw the darker
side of Henry Jekyll's nature. At least he knew from experience how the Enfields of the world exact retribution
from the Hydes for acts which they consider alien to their
codes of conscience.

There is about all of Stevenson's work an energy that
belies the fact that he was suffering from tuberculosis, and
a professionalism that utterly conceals the fact that he
found it very difficult to summon the strength to write on
some occasions. His novels and stories never seem to be
the product of a frail man. But, looking deeper, some
critics have suggested that his interest in dark themes,
such as we encounter in *Dr. Jekyll and Mr. Hyde* and the
short story of "Markheim," for example, may be traced
to the occasional brooding of a man whose body from
time to time reminded him of his mortality.

A few critics have suggested that the name of Stevenson's villain, Hyde, must be derived from the Rev. Dr.
C. M. Hyde of Honolulu to whom Stevenson wrote a letter
bristling with invective (from Sydney, February 25, 1890)
after the clergyman had attacked a Father Damien, a mis-
sionary who had heroically brought both the Gospel and
medical care to the lepers. However, we have to pay
attention to the date of the publication of *Dr. Jekyll and
Mr. Hyde.* It appeared as a shilling paperback before the
end of 1885 and was re-issued in January of the next
year to great acclaim. *The Times* gave it an enthusiastic
review. A sermon based on the story was preached at St.

Paul's Cathedral. In six months 40,000 copies of the book
had been sold—just what Stevenson needed. Dashing it
off, he had said: "I drive on with Jekyll; bankruptcy at
my heels." But all that was long before the incident about
Father Damien and Stevenson's impassioned defense of
him.

It was characteristic of Stevenson to rush from the success of *Dr. Jekyll and Mr. Hyde* to something else so fast
that he forgot to sell the American rights to the book.
It was pirated in this country and, though it sold perhaps
a quarter of a million copies here during the author's
lifetime, he never received a penny of American money
for it. Of course, Stevenson did not live to benefit from
film rights or television exploitation and never knew what
profits Walt Disney and others reaped from his works.
The man who asked publisher McClure for $800 for a
sequel to *Kidnapped*—he was given $8,000 and told to
smarten up—may not have cared.

He did care very much, however, that the message of
Dr. Jekyll and Mr. Hyde was widely disseminated, largely
among those who would never have picked up a work on
theology or psychology and whom the very word "meta-
physics" would frighten off. Though Stevenson claimed to
be one of the apostles of "art for art's sake," a popular
movement in his time, the Calvinist conscience that clung
to him long after he had become a secret agnostic could
never have allowed him to write a sheer piece of enter-
tainment wholly devoid of social significance. He was, un-
derneath, a Scottish "dominie," a teacher as well as an
artist. That somehow he was able to bring up from his
subconscious something that made him clearly see, though
not espouse, the creed of the demonic Mr. Hyde does not
contradict the fact that his was a delicate conscience, occasionally as agonized as that of the good Dr. Jekyll. If
one could thrill the public and make money at it too—

fine. But one must also, Stevenson felt, do some good. That obligation had been dinned into him. He had been taught from his youth that man consisted of evil, wild urges, kept in control only by dint of great effort, ever threatening to burst out. It was in conquering this evil side of one's nature, he was told, that the virtuous life was achieved. One recalls that Markheim, in the story of that name, having committed a brutal murder and having had his very own likeness rise up to taunt and revile him, finally sends for the police "with a tender triumph," and undergoes "a wonderful and lovely change" in deciding to confess his guilt. The evil side of human nature seems in *Dr. Jekyll and Mr. Hyde* to be far more destructive and far less predictable, the alter ego of the doctor being perhaps even more vividly drawn and even more vital in essence. But once again Stevenson's moral fable, *simplifying* life as he always stressed that fiction does, ends with virtue triumphant—or, at least, evil dead.

In June, 1888, in search of health, Stevenson and his family set sail for the South Seas. In the end they settled at Apia in Samoa. There the natives called him "Tusitala," which means "the Teller of Tales." After four happy years, he died. On his tombstone was engraved part of the requiem he had written for himself, all the battle with good and evil over, all the doubts stilled, all the moral ambiguities dissolved:

Under the wide and starry sky,
Dig the grave and let me lie.
Glad did I live and gladly die,
    And I laid me down with a will.

This be the verse you grave for me:
Here he lies where he longed to be;
Home is the sailor, home from the sea,
    And the hunter home from the hill.

HISTORICAL BACKGROUND

"In the small hours of one morning," Stevenson's wife
Fanny wrote, "I was awakened by cries of horror from
Louis. Thinking he had had a nightmare, I awakened
him. He said angrily, 'Why did you wake me? I was
dreaming a fine bogey tale.'" He remembered enough
of the dream, however, to sit up in his sickbed and write
a real "crawler," a horrifying tale. His son tells us that
Mrs. Stevenson objected that the story did not contain
enough moral message, that the allegory was not clearly
presented. Stevenson burned the first version of *Dr. Jekyll
and Mr. Hyde* and rewrote it.

As a student at the University of Edinburgh young
Stevenson gained a firsthand knowledge of low life. He
frequented the lowest dives and consorted with prostitutes,
being as debauched as was possible with a meager allowance of £6 a year. Flying in the face of convention, he
sowed his wild oats, going about with long hair and
dressed in a dandyish fashion that caused him to be nick-
named "Velvet Coat" by the denizens of Edinburgh's
brothels. In later life his outlook was too mature, his
wife too strict, and his time too occupied for him to haunt
the underworld of London, but he was able to create the
night world of the nefarious Mr. Hyde out of report and
gossip and to describe in sufficient detail the villain's dark
deeds in the London underworld. For a Victorian audience, fascinated with crime and criminals and familiar
with the slums of the city from the works of novelists
such as Charles Dickens, hints were enough. Readers
were more than willing to titillate themselves by imagin-
ing the background.

If Edward Hyde's evil character could be fleshed out in
the reader's imagination so also could that of Dr. Henry

Jekyll. In an age in which great advances were being made in medicine (such as the introduction of the antiseptic system, in 1860, by Joseph Lister), the good doctor in his laboratory was an ideal figure. Moreover, behind the respectable physician experimenting to serve humanity lurked traditions of evil which Stevenson could use: the infamous Dr. Frankenstein in Mary Shelley's celebrated novel, giving birth to a monster; the overreaching Dr. Faustus in Christopher Marlowe's play, seeking to know and do more "than heavenly power permits"; the anatomists who, to obtain bodies for dissection, consorted with criminals and ghouls, the case of Dr. Robert Knox in Edinburgh (who employed the Irish "resurrectionists" Burke and Hare to rob graves) being well known to Stevenson. Medicine, to the average person, seemed to be an arcane science in many respects, and the general reader was quite prepared for something of the science-fiction approach to issue from the mysterious laboratory of a "mad doctor." It was to Stevenson's credit that he built upon this appeal to produce a tale not simply eerily credible but truly significant and delivering a moral message.

Stevenson's tendency to incorporate psychological analysis was evident even in such adventure stories as his famous tale of Captain Kidd's treasure (*Treasure Island,* 1883) and the stories set against a Scottish background. The fragmentary *Weir of Hermiston,* which Henry James praised as a magnificent piece of creation but which Stevenson did not live to complete, shows his powers of psychological penetration at their very best. In it, the great Scottish judge Robert Macqueen, Lord Braxfield, appears as Adam Weir—and, like James Durie, *Master of Ballantrae,* and Mr. Hyde, he illustrates what Stevenson thought of as the incubus. "They are determinants of fate in those they dominate," writes Morton Zabel. "They belong to the lineage of Iago. They embody an energy which, though it works as evil, is vital beyond the capacities of virtue or goodness. They show a quicker life than men of conventional rectitude, and all three enact the sinister power that Stevenson felt such characters to possess—the fatality of the force of will in man's nature."

In our time such psychological insights would be discussed in terms of Freud, Jung, and other scientists. In Stevenson's time the great psychologists were not scientists but imaginative writers. The divided self in *Dr. Jekyll and Mr. Hyde* to some extent must have been derived from Dostoevsky and Dickens, Hawthorne and Melville and Poe. In their tradition, Stevenson enlisted the facility of his pen and the fecundity of his imagination to express deep-felt anxieties and intuitive solutions to the problems of his life, writing (as Ibsen said) to sit in judgment upon himself. In a literary tradition which extended back to the Middle Ages and far beyond, Stevenson clothed his message in allegory, putting a sugarcoating of excitement around his didactic pill of insight. It was good psychology, considerably ahead of the science of his period, that Stevenson presented in his "strange case" of what today we might describe as a schizophrenic personality. Modern psychoanalysts can tell us a good deal about the fictional personalities portrayed in the work and, in addition, something of the author's own personality as consciously or unconsciously revealed in his fiction. Of some of their interpretations and findings Stevenson himself might be leery, but he instinctively recognized the truths about human character which he used as the wellsprings of action in his thrilling tale and he knew also that it was "good psychology" to wrap his findings in a gripping story that would hold the attention of the reader, fix its scenes and details in his mind, and haunt his memory until such time as the full import of the message could be grasped.

Victorian readers would not have examined *Dr. Jekyll and Mr. Hyde* in terms of Freud's "id," "ego," and "superego." But they understood, whatever vocabulary of dementia they used to describe the phenomena, the split personality, the warring of contradictory urges within the human breast, the fact that a single person could vacillate dramatically between radically different mental states (manic and depressive, for instance). In *Dr. Jekyll and Mr. Hyde,* "both moral allegory and thriller," they saw psychological reality and sensed, with pleasure, that they were being instructed and improved at the same time that they were being thrilled and entertained by a "rattling good yarn." It was the best of both possible worlds.

The Victorians sought the same combination of suspense with morality in the drama. Their melodramas may have lacked the subtlety of the moral ambiguities that Stevenson habitually wrote about but they defended themselves against the charge of mere escapism by contending that their deep-dyed villains and their pure heroines and, indeed, all their stereotyped characters and situations provided moral uplift and good example. *Dr. Jekyll and Mr. Hyde* was, of course, even better suited to the cinema (where John Barrymore and later Spencer Tracy changed from the good doctor into the leering horror right before our very eyes, thanks to the magic of stop-motion photography), but it was also perfect for the Victorian stage. Richard Mansfield (1857–1907), "the foremost American actor of his time," as the *Oxford Companion to American Literature* calls him, played the dual role in an adaptation of Stevenson's story to great acclaim.

It would not be difficult to connect other features of Stevenson's story with literary antecedents. To cite one example: the emphasis in *Dr. Jekyll and Mr. Hyde* upon letters (especially ones not to be opened until after someone's death) and wills and other papers from the deceased recalls the epistolary novels so popular during the eighteenth century, though Stevenson was wise enough to present his action more directly. Moreover, there were the stories told through such devices as the "papers" of Dr. Watson (who gave us records of the adventures of Sherlock Holmes) and "the journal of Jonathan Harker" (through which we get much of the story of Dracula). Indeed *Dr. Jekyll and Mr. Hyde* was a milestone in the long development of horror and mystery stories which yielded works as different as the Gothic romances of Matthew "Monk" Lewis, the detective stories of Wilkie Collins and his literary heirs, the science fiction which in our time has ranged from the silliest BEM (or bug-eyed monster) escapism to highly significant social criticism.

The critic Desmond MacCarthy has called Stevenson "a little master." Compared to Dickens and other giants of English fiction in the "Great Tradition" of the nineteenth century which F. R. Leavis dates from novelist Jane Austen, Stevenson may be a minor figure, a writer who was on the verge of greater achievement (in *Weir of Hermiston*) when the frail body that had fought so valiantly through the years to contain the lively spirit finally succumbed to the illness that had so long stalked him. But, as *Chambers's Biographical Dictionary* says, after ennumerating Stevenson's many successes: "Nobody knew better than MacCarthy how much toil it takes to make a little master and how much delight he may convey to posterity." In *Dr. Jekyll and Mr. Hyde,* a little masterpiece constructed in the context of Victorian melodrama and didactic literature, Stevenson has given proof that he was able, even in a horror story, to do more than that awful little boy threatened in one of Dickens' novels: "to make your flesh creep." With the haunting story is a memorable message. Here are what the laureate Tennyson called "the abysmal depths of personality" plumbed to their depths in a moral tale.

Note: The page references on the following pages direct your attention to passages in the text (T for Top of page, M for Middle, and B for Bottom).

PICTORIAL BACKGROUND

It was reported by those who encountered them in their Sunday walks, that they said nothing, looked singularly dull, and would hail with obvious relief the appearance of a friend. For all that, the two men put the greatest store by these excursions, counted them the chief jewel of each week. . . . (p. 2B)

TWO BRITISH GENTLEMEN OUT FOR A STROLL—1870's

Two doors from one corner, on the left hand going east, the line was broken by the entry of a court; and just at that point, a certain sinister block of building thrust forward its gable on the street. It was two storeys high; showed no window, nothing but a door on the lower storey. . . . (p. 3M)

CHARLES R. MACAULEY'S VERSION OF MR. HYDE'S DOOR

"So we all set off, the doctor, and the child's father, and our friend and myself, and passed the rest of the night in my chambers; and next day . . . went in a body to the bank. I gave in the cheque myself, and said I had every reason to believe it was a forgery. Not a bit of it. The cheque was genuine." (p. 7M)

A NINETEENTH-CENTURY LONDON BANK

With that he blew out his candle, put on a great coat, and set forth in the direction of Cavendish Square, that citadel of medicine, where his friend, the great Dr. Lanyon, had his house and received his crowding patients. "If anyone knows, it will be Lanyon," he had thought. (p. 12B)

A DISTINGUISHED LONDON HOME OF THE PERIOD

Mr. Utterson *stopped and knocked. A well-dressed, elderly servant opened the door.*

"*Is Dr. Jekyll at home, Poole?*" *asked the lawyer.*

"*I will see, Mr. Utterson,*" *said Poole, admitting the visitor, as he spoke, into a large, low-roofed, comfortable hall. . . .* (p. 21T)

A BUTLER ADMITTING A VISITOR—1800's

A fortnight later, by excellent good fortune, the doctor gave one of his pleasant dinners to some five or six old cronies, all intelligent, reputable men and all judges of good wine; and Mr. Utterson so contrived that he remained behind after the others had departed. (p. 25T)

DINNER PARTY—LONDON, 1880

At the horror of these sights and sounds, the maid fainted. It was two o'clock when she came to herself and called for the police. The murderer was gone long ago; but there lay his victim in the middle of the lane, incredibly mangled. (p. 31T)

POLICE ARRIVE TO INVESTIGATE A MURDER—1800's

The stick with which the deed had been done, although it was of some rare and very tough and heavy wood, had broken in the middle under the stress of this insensate cruelty; and one splintered half had rolled in the neighbouring gutter—the other, without doubt, had been carried away by the murderer. (p. 31M)

THE MOVIE VERSION OF THE PREVIOUS SCENE, DEPICTING THE MURDER OF SIR DANVERS CAREW
(Reprinted with permission of Metro-Goldwyn-Mayer)

It was by this time about nine in the morning, and the first fog of the season. A great chocolate-coloured pall lowered over heaven, but the wind was continually charging and routing these embattled vapours; so that . . . Mr. Utterson beheld a marvelous number of degrees and hues of twilight. . . . (p. 32B)

DAYTIME FOG IN LONDON—1876

As the cab drew up before the address indicated, the fog lifted a little and showed him a dingy street, a gin palace, a low French eating house, a shop for the retail of penny numbers and twopenny salads, many ragged children huddled in the doorways. . . . *(p. 33B)*

A DINGY STREET IN LONDON—LATE 1800's

. . . *the other half of the stick was found behind the door; and as this clinched his suspicions, the officer declared himself delighted. A visit to the bank, where several thousand pounds were found to be lying to the murderer's credit, completed his gratification. (p. 35M)*

A LONDON POLICEMAN—1800's

It was late in the afternoon when Mr. Utterson found his way to Dr. Jekyll's door, where he was at once admitted by Poole, and carried down by the kitchen offices and across a yard which had once been a garden, to the building which was indifferently known as the laboratory. . . . (p. 37T)

A LABORATORY—LATE 1800's

The newsboys, as he went, were crying themselves hoarse along the footways: "Special edition. Shocking murder of an M. P." That was the funeral oration of one friend and client; and he could not help a certain apprehension lest the good name of another should be sucked down in the eddy of the scandal. (p. 41M)

NEWSBOYS HAWKING THEIR WARES—1871

*The court was very cool and a little damp, and full of pre-
mature twilight, although the sky, high up overhead, was
still bright with sunset. The middle one of the three windows
was half-way open; and sitting close beside it . . . like some
disconsolate prisoner, Utterson saw Dr. Jekyll. (p. 54T)*

COURTYARD OF A LONDON HOUSE—1800's

. . . the door was opened on the chain; and a voice asked from within, "Is that you, Poole?"

"It's all right," said Poole. "Open the door."

The hall, when they entered it, was brightly lighted up . . . the whole of the servants, men and women, stood huddled together like a flock of sheep. (p. 59B)

ENTRANCE HALL—LONDON, LATE 1800's

"Well, sir, every day, ay, and twice and thrice in the same day, there have been orders and complaints, and I have been sent flying to all the wholesale chemists in town. Every time I brought the stuff back, there would be another paper telling me to return it, because it was not pure...." (p. 62B)

A CHEMIST'S SHOP—1800's

The footman came at the summons, very white and nervous.
"Put yourself together, Bradshaw," said the lawyer. "This
suspense, I know, is telling upon all of you; but it is now our
intention to make an end of it." (p. 67B)

A FOOTMAN—1800's

The lawyer put it in his pocket. "I would say nothing of this paper. If your master has fled or is dead, we may at least save his credit. It is now ten; I must go home and read these documents in quiet; but I shall be back before midnight, when we shall send for the police." (p. 75B)

READING THE FATAL DOCUMENTS

In the 1941 adaptation of Stevenson's famous thriller, Metro-Goldwyn-Mayer script writers thought it necessary to introduce romantic elements into the story. One of these was Ivy Pearson, presumably a bar girl Mr. Hyde met during his nocturnal visits in search of "one of my adventures." (p. 100M)

INGRID BERGMAN AS IVY PEARSON
(Reprinted with permission of Metro-Goldwyn-Mayer)

Another female character who sprang from the fertile imaginations of the movie script writers was a young lady named Beatrix. Here she is pictured speaking to Dr. Jekyll: "I don't want to leave you—ever!"

SPENCER TRACY AS DR. JEKYLL AND
LANA TURNER AS BEATRIX
(Reprinted with permission of Metro-Goldwyn-Mayer)

It was a fine, clear, January day, wet under foot where the frost had melted, but cloudless overhead; and the Regent's Park was full of winter chirrupings and sweet with spring odours. I sat in the sun on a bench; the animal within me licking the chops of memory; the spiritual side a little drowsed. . . . (p. 108B)

REGENT'S PARK—LONDON, 1800's

Thereupon, I arranged my clothes as best I could, and summoning a passing hansom, drove to an hotel in Portland Street, the name of which I chanced to remember. At my appearance . . . the driver could not conceal his mirth. I gnashed my teeth upon him with a gust of devilish fury. . . . (p. 110M)

A CHEAP LONDON HOTEL—1800's

Thenceforward, he sat all day over the fire in the private room, gnawing his nails; there he dined, sitting alone with his fears, the waiter visibly quailing before his eye; and thence, when the night was fully come, he set forth in the corner of a closed cab, and was driven to and fro about the streets of the city. (p. 111M)

CABS IN A LONDON STREET—1800's

VISUAL GLOSSARY

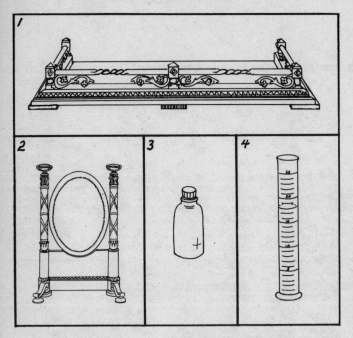

1–fender (p. 21B)
2–cheval-glass (p. 38T)
3–phial (p. 71T)
4–graduated glass
    (p. 86T)

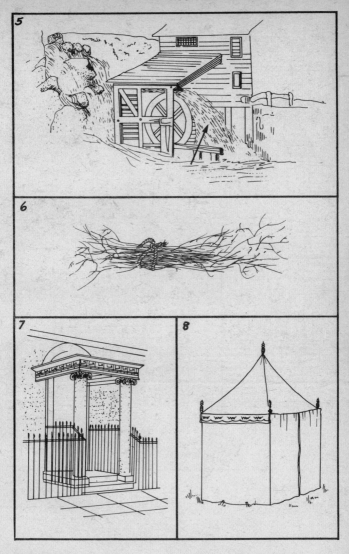

5—millrace (p. 94T)   7—portico (p. 82B)
6—faggots (p. 92T)   8—pavilion (p. 92M)

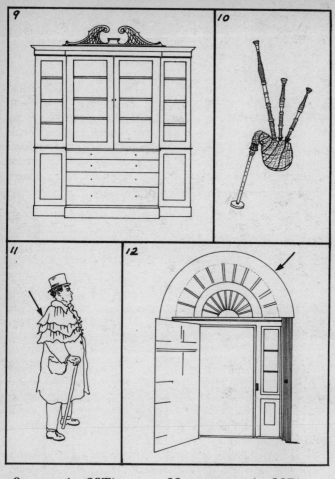

9–press (p. 38T)   11–greatcoat (p. 12B)
10–bagpipe (p. 6T)   12–fanlight (p. 21T)

LITERARY ALLUSIONS AND NOTES

Cain's heresy (p. 1B):
This biblical reference is to Genesis 4:8–12. Cain had killed his brother Abel. When the Lord asked Cain where his brother was, Cain replied, "I know not. Am I my brother's keeper?" Mr. Utterson often defended criminals in court and befriended them instead of trying to reform them. He explained that he believed in Cain's improper doctrine, felt that he was not the keeper of his fellowmen, and let them continue on their evil ways.

Juggernaut (p. 5M):
In the Hindu religion, Juggernaut is a form of the incarnation of Vishnu, a supreme deity. Juggernaut's image and those of his brother and sister were mounted each summer on an enormous cart and dragged by thousands of pilgrims to a summer home. Religious zealots would often hurl themselves to death beneath the moving wheels of the huge cart. Mr. Enfield said that, as Mr. Hyde trampled over the child's body, he seemed like the Juggernaut's cart crushing victims beneath its wheels.

view halloa (p. 5M):
This is an expression used in the popular British sport of fox hunting. A *view halloa* is a shout uttered by a huntsman when he sees the fox break cover and come into the open. Here Mr. Enfield gave the shout as a signal that he had seen the culprit and would try to catch him.

harpies (p. 6M):
In Greek mythology, the Harpies were birds with women's faces who were known as "Snatchers" because they would snatch the souls away from the living. The neighborhood women seemed as wild and ravenous as the Harpies as they struggled to get their hands on the man who had trampled the child.

apocryphal (p. 7M):
This word is derived from the *Apochrypha,* those parts of the Bible which were regarded as of doubtful authorship

or authority. Mr. Enfield regards the "whole business" of
the cheque as false or at least questionable.

day of judgment (p. 8M):
This is regarded as the last day of the world, doomsday,
the day of accounting when the evil will suffer. Mr.
Enfield said that he had not tried to investigate Hyde's
house for he felt that asking questions might lead to the
discovery of hidden evil.

M.D., D.C.L., L.L.D., F.R.S., etc. (p. 11B):
The initials stand for Doctor of Medicine, Doctor of Civil
Law, Doctor of Laws, Fellow of the Royal Society. Here
the author indicated Dr. Jekyll's high educational attain-
ments and the recognition accorded him.

Damon and Pythias (p. 14T):
These were two Greek friends whose names are traditional-
ly used to characterize a perfect friendship. When Pythias
was sentenced to death in Sicily, Damon pledged himself as
a hostage so that Pythias might go home to arrange his
affairs. Pythias returned to redeem his friend and to meet
his death. The example of friendship was so striking that
both men were released. Dr. Lanyon said that, while he
and Dr. Jekyll had been close friends, their disagreements
about Dr. Jekyll's scientific theories were strong enough to
have separated even perfect friends like Damon and
Pythias.

labyrinths (p. 15B):
In Greek mythology, the Labyrinth was a maze constructed
by Daedalus to house the Minotaur, a monster. The maze
was so elaborately winding that, once a person entered it,
he could not find his way out but would have to continue
through the confusing pathways until he was devoured by
the Minotaur. When Mr. Utterson dozed, he seemed to see
the evil figure of Hyde moving through the winding mazes
of city streets, trampling children along the way.

Dr. Fell (p. 20B):
This is a reference to the famous jingle by Thomas Brown
(1663–1704) written as a free translation of Martial's
Epigram I, 33.

> I do not love thee, Dr. Fell;
> The reason why I cannot tell;
> But this alone I know full well,
> I do not love thee, Dr. Fell.

Trying to analyze his reason for loathing Mr. Hyde, Mr. Utterson asked himself whether his feeling might be just as hard to explain as the poet's reason for disliking Dr. Fell.

statute of limitations (p. 22B):

This is a law setting a certain time limit after which rights and wrongs may not be adjudicated in courts of law. Musing over Mr. Hyde's possible hold over Dr. Jekyll, Mr. Utterson wondered whether it might have to do with some wrong committed by Dr. Jekyll in his youth. In God's eyes, there is no statute of limitations, he mused, for God can always hold us accountable for our sins.

captives of Philippi (p. 96B):

This is a reference to the battle of Philippi (42 B.C.) as treated in Shakespeare's *Julius Caesar,* Act V. Cassius and Brutus, faced with defeat, killed themselves rather than be taken captive. Dr. Jekyll wrote that his chemical potion served to let loose whatever evil motives he had locked within himself just as the piercing swords let loose the lifeblood of Cassius and Brutus.

Babylonian finger on the wall (p. 102M):

In Daniel 5:5–25, a mysterious hand wrote "MENE, MENE, TEKEL, UPHARSIN" on the wall during a feast given by Belshazzar, king of Babylon. Daniel interpreted the words as a prophecy of the destruction of Belshazzar and his kingdom. We use the expression *handwriting on the wall* to mean "omen of doom." Dr. Jekyll wrote that, after he had changed into Mr. Hyde in his sleep without having drunk his potion, he began to feel his doom approaching just as was foretold by the handwriting on the wall.

CRITICAL EXCERPTS

For a sick man who died prematurely, Stevenson's literary output was astonishing in number and in variety: novels, short stories, poetry, criticism, essays, travel sketches, and even drama. All of his work was not of the same quality, of course. His reputation as a writer has gone through cycles of enthusiastic praise and scornful belittlement. His best works, nevertheless, have remained popular.

One aspect of Stevenson's work on which almost all critics agree is his style. They praise his diligence in seeking precisely the right word to express an idea, but you will note that some commentators find him overprecise and overrefined in that search.

1. *That is a point to note in Stevenson's equipment, that he was always very apt with the pen. Having turned writer in his youth, he remained a writer to the end. . . . If clarity is a virtue in writing . . . then Stevenson deserves praise for most admirable clarity. There is no difficulty of style. It is easy to read because it has so much grace, but it is also easy to understand because it is in a high degree explicit.*

Frank Swinnerton, *Robert Louis Stevenson, A Critical Study*, George H. Doran Company, 1923.

2. *Stevenson has suffered more than most from this new fashion of minimizing and finding fault. . . . They condemn him for being fastidious . . . for wasting time in trying to find the right word. . . . Now it is nonsense for anybody who pretends to like literature not to see the excellence of Stevenson's expression in this way. He does pick the words that make the picture he has of a particular thing.*

G. K. Chesterton, *Robert Louis Stevenson*, Sheed and Ward, 1955.

3. *The style in itself is a delight. The sentences have an etcher's precision. Varied as their cadences are and eerie as is the music they create, they drive on steadily with ever-mounting tension as they unfold their terrible story.*

> John Mason Brown, Introduction to *The Strange Case of Dr. Jekyll and Mr. Hyde,* The Limited Editions Club, 1952.

4. *The style has ease, suppleness, limpidity, felicity—every virtue save that of strength. . . . One has to seek far to find so perfect a use of the English language to convey the simpler emotions and ideas of life.*

> J. W. Cunliffe, *English Literature during the Last Half-Century,* The Macmillan Company, 1923.

5. *Stevenson was a most careful and laborious artificer in words, fastidious to the verge of overrefinement in the niceties of style. . . . He excels in pictorial power. His stories abound in scenes which are indelibly stamped on the imagination.*

> Henry S. Pancoast, *An Introduction to English Literature,* Henry Holt and Company, 1907.

6. *Stevenson is a born writer with a clear, exact, nervous, and smooth style.*

> Emile Legouis and Louis Cazamian, *A History of English Literature,* The Macmillan Company, 1930.

7. *Perhaps as far as literature is concerned, Stevenson's highest fame will rest upon his style. . . . He was able to fashion one of the distinctive styles in English. It is fluid, nervous, musical, approaching perfection in its use of* le mot unique. *There are those who profess to find it too ornate and*

too much prettified and who apply the word precieuse *with
some contempt. If Stevenson's style appears overnice and
overrefined, it is because one fashion today is for stalwart
and even shapeless composition. There is no amorphous
writing in Stevenson; he risked the charge of being too sugary,
never of lacking manner. Time and again he surprises by
the uncanny selection of the best word, a grace that shows at
its best in his descriptions.*

> Grant C. Knight, *The Novel in
> English,* Farrar and Rinehart, Inc.,
> 1935.

8. *Stevenson's enormous popularity, partly the result of his
narrative gift but also the reward of his style, which has an
unusual and very personal grace and charm (and some of
his sourer critics might try to learn something from it before
dismissing it as a mere trick), has now lasted a long time, so
long that only prejudice would deny this continuing popularity a hard core of genuine literary acceptance.*

> J. B. Priestley, *Literature and West-
> ern Man,* Harper and Brothers,
> 1960.

To evaluate Stevenson's skill in choice of language, review some of his descriptions. Consider his treatment of
London weather: the full moon in the clear night (p. 29M)
by means of which the maid witnessed the murder: the murky
fog (p. 32T) through which Mr. Utterson drove, as in a
nightmare, (p. 33M) to the home of Mr. Hyde (p. 33B); the
contrast between Mr. Utterson's cheerful hearthside and the
fog outside (pp. 41B–42T); the cold and windy night
(pp. 58B–59T) when Mr. Utterson accompanied Poole to
investigate Dr. Jekyll's disappearance; the darkness and stillness (p. 68B) as Mr. Utterson and Poole prepared to
break into Dr. Jekyll's room; and the clear day in Regent's
Park (p. 108B) when Dr. Jekyll was transformed in public
without benefit of his potion. (It may be of interest to note

here that some critics believe that passages like these influenced Sir Arthur Conan Doyle to use similar weather descriptions in the settings for his eerie Sherlock Holmes stories.)

Among the adverse criticisms of Stevenson's work is a charge of "thinness." Because he wrote so much and at times at great speed, he laid himself open to complaints that he stressed action at the expense of character, that he concentrated on main points at the expense of details, and that much of his work was superficial without the benefits of extended analysis or deep thinking. On the other hand, there are those critics who praise his conciseness, economy of words, and simplicity.

9. *Stevenson is wan and slight. He had no penetration. He was not a thinker.*

> Knight, *The Novel in English.*

10. *In* Dr. Jekyll and Mr. Hyde *we find Stevenson attracted . . . by the problems of the subconscious. . . . The case of a dual personality is not studied with superior subtlety, but it is brought home to our imaginations with striking efficiency.*

> Legouis and Cazamian, *A History of English Literature.*

11. Dr. Jekyll and Mr. Hyde *owes its popularity to the striking nature of its theme and the picturesque boldness with which it is treated. As an allegory it does not stand up very well to detailed examination, but this is unimportant beside the fact that the ringing strokes employed by Stevenson in fashioning the story give it extraordinary vigor; it is a rough-hewn and crude piece of work, but as narrative it is extremely well-managed. . . . There is no inevitability in the decisions taken by the characters and no moral implication. Even Dr. Jekyll is not shown as taking his fateful decision to experiment with disassociation as a result of any characteristic weakness of character; his motives are indicated with the utmost*

brevity; the interest lies in the action only, and not in its relation to character.

> David Daiches, *Robert Louis Stevenson,* New Directions, 1947.

12. *The tale is a "masterpiece of concision" as Henry James said, and much of its swift dramatic power derives from its skilled economy of word and incident.*

> John Hampden, Introduction to *Dr. Jekyll and Mr. Hyde,* The Folio Society, 1948.

13. *The real defect of Stevenson as a writer . . . was that he simplified so much that he lost some of the comfortable complexity of real life. He treated everything with an economy of detail and a suppression of irrelevance which had at last something about it stark and unnatural. . . . He never says anything needlessly; above all he never says anything twice. . . . Stevenson's work has its faults, like other good work; and its chief deficiency does appear in a certain defect of thinness, which is produced by this instinct for hard simplification.*

> Chesterton, *Robert Louis Stevenson.*

14. *He is a master of narrative, with an unerring sense of the essential, enabling ruthless rejection of the temptation to digressive embellishment; he is evidently fascinated, not only by the analysis of character—as in* Dr. Jekyll and Mr. Hyde—*but also in the play of character upon character.*

> Malcolm Elwin, *The Strange Case of Robert Louis Stevenson,* McDonald and Company, 1950.

Insofar as Stevenson's handling of character is concerned, the critics disagree rather sharply. He is charged with a lack of "penetration," too much brevity in defining motives, and, as noted before, a general "thinness" in treatment. However, Elwin speaks of Stevenson's fascination by the analysis of character and the "play of character upon character." How deeply did the author probe? This is the basic question. Stevenson *described* his people, but did he get inside them, as modern novelists usually do?

Some criticism of details in the book appeared soon after publication.

15. *Some of the objections made to the story seem unfounded. Thus, the complaint is made that in his own way Jekyll was as bad as Hyde, if not worse. No doubt this is true from the point of view of a skeptical modern intellectual, but it was not true for Stevenson's audience who would consider the prosperous, fashionable, luxurious, and rather smug doctor a fulfillment of their ideas of respectability. Again, there is the objection that the potion which causes the physical changes of Jekyll and Hyde is medically impossible. Of course it is. . . . In these tales of fantasy, we must accept impossible causes of remarkable effects. . . . Indeed, if we are looking for subsidiary allegories here, we might find one in the ulti- mate failure of the potion—symbolizing the ultimate failure of Science either to resolve Man's destiny or to alleviate his lot. There are minor points of more validity. Thus, at the time of publication, Frederick Myers wrote Stevenson and noted several, including the now famous one where Hyde, about to drink the potion in Lanyon's presence, conjures him to silence "under the seal of our profession" (p. 87M). Obviously Dr. Lanyon's instant and indignant answer would have been: "You're not a doctor!" Stevenson could easily have corrected this, but did not, and after all what do such trifles matter? I should guess that on a first reading 99 people out of 100 never notice them. Other minor objections raised are that the police inquiries into the murder of Sir Danvers would certainly have connected Hyde with Jekyll, and the doctor would have had to answer some very embarrassing questions. . . . And surely the fiendishly malicious Hyde would hardly have committed*

*suicide so tamely. . . . The answer to all such objections is
that the story achieved its aim of interesting readers.*

> Richard Aldington, *Portrait of a
> Rebel,* Evans Brothers, Ltd., 1957.

16. *John Aldington Symonds wrote to Stevenson: "The suicide end of Jekyll . . . is too commonplace. Dr. Jekyll ought
to have given himself up to justice. This would have vindi-
cated the sense of human dignity which is so horribly outraged
in your book.*

> John A. Steuart, *Robert Louis Ste-
> venson: A Critical Biography,*
> Little, Brown, and Company, 1924.

17. *As Stevenson remarked, many critics censured "the business of the powders. . . ." Opinion continues divided concern-
ing this device. . . . Mr. Compton Mackenzie considers that
"today that drug handicaps the story with an old-fashioned
artificiality"; Mr. Desmond MacCarthy believes that the
worlds of romance and reality are related, but to mix them
up is fatal and that Stevenson's instinct to keep the magic
potion was therefore sound. Acceptance of Mr. MacCarthy's
distinction between "the worlds of romance and reality"
requires the reader of* Jekyll and Hyde *to ignore the allegory
in appreciation of the story—to regard it . . . as "a masterpiece of the terrible and grotesque with an unobtrusive and
salutary moral." For most of the thousands contributing to
the book's immediate popular success, the moral was not
"unobtrusive"; the allegory was the story's chief attraction,
being interpreted as a sensationally daring satire on contem-
porary morality. . . . A canon of St. Paul's seized upon the
the allegory as the text for a sermon, and lesser clergy followed suit. In Victorian England, publicity from the pulpit
was the most influential form of advertisement; in Gosse's
words,* Jekyll and Hyde *instantly became the subject of dis-
cussion in every class of lettered society, and it is from the
moment of its publication that Stevenson, already passionately*

*admired within a comparatively narrow circle, began to take
a foremost place in the general world of letters.*

Elwin, *The Strange Case of Robert
Louis Stevenson.*

Other questions have been raised about the book. Knowing
that Stevenson was a rebel—against his father's strict religious
doctrines, against his father's choice of profession for him,
and against Victorian standards of behavior—many critics
wonder how much of Dr. Jekyll's double self might have been
autobiographical.

18. *Of all his writing, Stevenson said, the one he considered
the worst was* Dr. Jekyll and Mr. Hyde. *The most famous of
his stories, the pot of gold, the work which made him a
theme for the pulpit—leading to affluence, leading to moral
reputation—was the writing he regarded as a failure! How
strange! How extraordinary! How very, very simple! How
pathetically obvious! . . . Here was a confession whose significance can only now be fully understood. The dramatic tale
of the duality of man's nature, thrilling for the multitude and
ethically inspiring for the elect, had, in its original form, been
quite another piece of work. Just what had been the first conception and the first execution must remain forever unknown.*

George S. Hellman, *The True Stevenson*, Little, Brown, and Company, 1925.

19. *In 1896, W. J. Dawson wrote: "A piece of writing like
this is a unique achievement in the art of letters. It is really
comparable with nothing else; it stands alone. And it is conclusive evidence of that subtlety and force of spiritual genius
which gives Stevenson a place apart . . . as an interpreter of
the deepest things of the human soul."*

J. A. Hammerton, *Stevensoniana,*
John Grant, 1910.

20. *If this* Strange Case *were no more than the "shocker"
which Stevenson first planned, it would still be a remarkable
novel, for the originality of the idea is matched by the skill
with which tension is added to mystery almost to the end.
But it is far more than that. The title has become proverbial
. . . because it touches some of the most primitive chords of
feeling; there is no more forceful presentation of that duality
in man's nature of which every human being is painfully
aware.*

Hampden, Introduction to *Dr. Jekyll and Mr. Hyde.*

A summary view of the book brings this section to a close.

21. *It was* The Strange Case of Dr. Jekyll and Mr. Hyde
*which in both England and America had done the most to
establish his reputation. . . . The truest measure of the
story's popularity was that the names in its title had already
passed into the language, where they have remained ever
since as synonyms for good and evil and a split personality.
. . .* Dr. Jekyll and Mr. Hyde *remains in a class by itself. It is
a* tour de force *of amazing virtuosity. Stevenson was as a
prose artist one of the most adroit technicians ever to have
employed the English language. . . . The narrative is built and
advanced with a marvelous awareness of every thrill and
shudder its gruesome tale contains. It is melodrama, sul-
phurous and appalling, which by the sheer black magic of its
telling is lifted into literature.*

Brown, Introduction to *The Strange
Case of Dr. Jekyll and Mr. Hyde.*

THE LAST NIGHT

MR. UTTERSON was sitting by his fireside one evening after dinner, when he was surprised to receive a visit from Poole.

"Bless me, Poole, what brings you here?" he cried; and then taking a second look at him, "What ails you?" he added; "is the doctor ill?"

"Mr. Utterson," said the man, "there is something wrong."

"Take a seat, and here is a glass of wine for you," said the lawyer. "Now, take your time, and tell me plainly what you want."

"You know the doctor's ways, sir," replied Poole, "and how he shuts himself up. Well, he's shut up again in the cabinet; and I don't like it, sir—I wish I may die if I like it. Mr. Utterson, sir, I'm afraid."

"Now, my good man," said the lawyer, "be explicit. What are you afraid of?"

"I've been afraid for about a week," returned Poole, doggedly disregarding the question, "and I can bear it no more."

The man's appearance amply bore out his words; his manner was altered for the worse; and except for the moment when he had first announced his terror, he had not once looked the lawyer in the face. Even now, he sat with the glass of wine untasted on his knee, and his eyes directed to a corner of the floor. "I can bear it no more," he repeated.

"Come," said the lawyer, "I see you have some good reason, Poole; I see there is something seriously amiss. Try to tell me what it is."

"I think there's been foul play," said Poole, hoarsely.

"Foul play!" cried the lawyer, a good deal frightened and rather inclined to be irritated in consequence. "What foul play! What does the man mean?"

"I daren't say, sir," was the answer; "but will you come along with me and see for yourself?"

Mr. Utterson's only answer was to rise and get his hat and greatcoat; but he observed with wonder the greatness of the relief that appeared upon the butler's face, and perhaps with no less, that the wine was still untasted when he set it down to follow.

It was a wild, cold, seasonable night of March, with a pale moon, lying on her back as though the wind had tilted her, and flying wrack of the most diaphanous and lawny texture. The wind made talking difficult, and flecked the blood into the face. It seemed to have swept the streets unusually bare of passengers, besides; for Mr. Utterson thought he had never seen that part of London so deserted. He could have wished it otherwise; never in his life had he been conscious of so sharp a wish to see and touch his fellow-creatures; for struggle as he might, there was borne in upon his mind a crushing anticipation of calamity. The square, when they got there, was full of wind and dust, and the thin trees in the garden were lashing themselves along the railing. Poole, who had kept all the way a pace or two ahead, now pulled up in the middle of the pavement, and in spite of the biting weather, took off his hat and mopped his brow with a red pocket handkerchief. But for all the hurry of his coming, these were not the dews of exertion that he wiped away, but the moisture of some strangling anguish; for his face was white and his voice, when he spoke, harsh and broken.

"Well, sir," he said, "here we are, and God grant there be nothing wrong."

"Amen, Poole," said the lawyer.

Thereupon the servant knocked in a very guarded manner; the door was opened on the chain; and a voice asked from within, "Is that you, Poole?"

"It's all right," said Poole. "Open the door."

The hall, when they entered it, was brightly

lighted up; the fire was built high; and about the hearth the whole of the servants, men and women, stood huddled together like a flock of sheep. At the sight of Mr. Utterson, the housemaid broke into hysterical whimpering; and the cook, crying out "Bless God! it's Mr. Utterson," ran forward as if to take him in her arms.

"What, what? Are you all here?" said the lawyer peevishly. "Very irregular, very unseemly; your master would be far from pleased."

"They're all afraid," said Poole.

Blank silence followed, no one protesting; only the maid lifted her voice and now wept loudly.

"Hold your tongue!" Poole said to her, with a ferocity of accent that testified to his own jangled nerves; and indeed, when the girl had so suddenly raised the note of her lamentation, they had all started and turned towards the inner door with faces of dreadful expectation. "And now," continued the butler, addressing the knife-boy, "reach me a candle, and we'll get this through hands at once." And then he begged Mr. Utterson to follow him, and led the way to the back garden.

"Now, sir," said he, "you come as gently as you can. I want you to hear, and I don't want you to be heard. And see here, sir, if by any chance he was to ask you in, don't go."

Mr. Utterson's nerves, at this unlooked-for termination, gave a jerk that nearly threw him from balance; but he recollected his courage and followed the butler into the laboratory building through the surgical theatre, with its lumber of crates and bottles, to the foot of the stair. Here Poole motioned him to stand on one side and listen; while he himself, setting down the candle and making a great and obvious call on his resolution, mounted the steps and knocked with a somewhat uncertain hand on the red baize of the cabinet door.

"Mr. Utterson, sir, asking to see you," he called; and even as he did so, once more violently signed to the lawyer to give ear.

A voice answered from within: "Tell him I cannot see anyone," it said complainingly.

"Thank you, sir," said Poole, with a note of something like triumph in his voice; and taking up his candle, he led Mr. Utterson back across the yard and into the great kitchen, where the fire was out and the beetles were leaping on the floor.

"Sir," he said, looking Mr. Utterson in the eyes, "was that my master's voice?"

"It seems much changed," replied the lawyer, very pale, but giving look for look.

"Changed? Well, yes, I think so," said the butler. "Have I been twenty years in this man's house, to be deceived about his voice? No, sir;

master's made away with; he was made away with eight days ago, when we heard him cry out upon the name of God; and *who's* in there instead of him, and *why* it stays there, is a thing that cries to Heaven, Mr. Utterson!"

"This is a very strange tale, Poole; this is rather a wild tale, my man," said Mr. Utterson, biting his finger. "Suppose it were as you suppose, supposing Dr. Jekyll to have been—well, murdered, what could induce the murderer to stay? That won't hold water; it doesn't commend itself to reason."

"Well, Mr. Utterson, you are a hard man to satisfy, but I'll do it yet," said Poole. "All this last week (you must know) him, or it, whatever it is that lives in that cabinet, has been crying night and day for some sort of medicine and cannot get it to his mind. It was sometimes his way—the master's, that is—to write his orders on a sheet of paper and throw it on the stair. We've had nothing else this week back; nothing but papers, and a closed door, and the very meals left there to be smuggled in when nobody was looking. Well, sir, every day, ay, and twice and thrice in the same day, there have been orders and complaints, and I have been sent flying to all the wholesale chemists in town. Every time I brought the stuff back, there would be another paper telling me to return it, because it was not pure, and another order to a different firm. This drug is wanted bitter bad, sir, whatever for."

"Have you any of these papers?" asked Mr. Utterson.

Poole felt in his pocket and handed out a crumpled note, which the lawyer, bending nearer to the candle, carefully examined. Its contents ran thus: "Dr. Jekyll presents his compliments to Messrs. Maw. He assures them that their last sample is impure and quite useless for his present purpose. In the year 18—, Dr. J. purchased a somewhat large quantity from Messrs. M. He now begs them to search with most sedulous care, and should any of the same quality be left, to forward it to him at once. Expense is no consideration. The importance of this to Dr. J. can hardly be exaggerated." So far the letter had run composedly enough, but here with a sudden splutter of the pen, the writer's emotion had broken loose. "For God's sake," he added, "find me some of the old."

"This is a strange note," said Mr. Utterson; and then sharply, "How do you come to have it open?"

"The man at Maw's was main angry, sir, and he threw it back to me like so much dirt," returned Poole.

"This is unquestionably the doctor's hand, do you know?" resumed the lawyer.

"I thought it looked like it," said the servant

rather sulkily; and then, with another voice, "But what matters hand of write?" he said. "I've seen him!"

"Seen him?" repeated Mr. Utterson. "Well?"

"That's it!" said Poole. "It was this way. I came suddenly into the theatre from the garden. It seems he had slipped out to look for this drug or whatever it is; for the cabinet door was open, and there he was at the far end of the room digging among the crates. He looked up when I came in, gave a kind of cry, and whipped upstairs into the cabinet. It was but for one minute that I saw him, but the hair stood upon my head like quills. Sir, if that was my master, why had he a mask upon his face? If it was my master, why did he cry out like a rat, and run from me? I have served long enough. And then . . ." The man paused and passed his hand over his face.

"These are all very strange circumstances," said Mr. Utterson, "but I think I begin to see daylight. Your master, Poole, is plainly seized with one of those maladies that both torture and deform the sufferer; hence, for aught I know, the alteration of his voice; hence the mask and the avoidance of his friends; hence his eagerness to find this drug, by means of which the poor soul retains some hope of ultimate recovery—God grant that he be not deceived! There is my explanation; it is sad enough, Poole, ay, and appalling to consider; but it is plain and natural, hangs well together, and delivers us from all exorbitant alarms."

"Sir," said the butler, turning to a sort of mottled pallor, "that thing was not my master, and there's the truth. "My master"—here he looked round him and began to whisper—"is a tall, fine build of a man, and this was more of a dwarf." Utterson attempted to protest. "O, sir," cried Poole, "do you think I do not know my master after twenty years? Do you think I do not know where his head comes to in the cabinet door, where I saw him every morning of my life? No, sir, that thing in the mask was never Dr. Jekyll—God knows what it was, but it was never Dr. Jekyll; and it is the belief of my heart that there was murder done."

"Poole," replied the lawyer, "if you say that, it will become my duty to make certain. Much as I desire to spare your master's feelings, much as I am puzzled by this note which seems to prove him to be still alive, I shall consider it my duty to break in that door."

"Ah, Mr. Utterson, that's talking!" cried the butler.

"And now comes the second question," resumed Utterson: "Who is going to do it?"

"Why, you and me, sir," was the undaunted reply.

"That's very well said," returned the lawyer; "and whatever comes of it, I shall make it my business to see you are no loser."

"There is an axe in the theatre," continued Poole; "and you might take the kitchen poker for yourself."

The lawyer took that rude but weighty instrument into his hand, and balanced it. "Do you know, Poole," he said, looking up, "that you and I are about to place ourselves in a position of some peril?"

"You may say so, sir, indeed," returned the butler.

"It is well, then, that we should be frank," said the other. "We both think more than we have said; let us make a clean breast. This masked figure that you saw, did you recognise it?"

"Well, sir, it went so quick, and the creature was so doubled up, that I could hardly swear to that," was the answer. "But if you mean, was it Mr. Hyde?—why, yes, I think it was! You see, it was much of the same bigness; and it had the same quick, light way with it; and then who else could have got in by the laboratory door? You have not forgot, sir, that at the time of the murder he had still the key with him? But that's not all. I don't know, Mr. Utterson, if you ever met this Mr. Hyde?"

"Yes," said the lawyer, "I once spoke with him."

"Then you must know as well as the rest of us that there was something queer about that gentleman—something that gave a man a turn—I don't know rightly how to say it, sir, beyond this: that you felt in your marrow kind of cold and thin."

"I own I felt something of what you describe," said Mr. Utterson.

"Quite so, sir," returned Poole. "Well, when that masked thing like a monkey jumped from among the chemicals and whipped into the cabinet, it went down my spine like ice. O, I know it's not evidence, Mr. Utterson; I'm book-learned enough for that; but a man has his feelings, and I give you my bible-word it was Mr. Hyde!"

"Ay, ay," said the lawyer. "My fears incline to the same point. Evil, I fear, founded—evil was sure to come—of that connection. Ay truly, I believe you; I believe poor Harry is killed; and I believe his murderer (for what purpose, God alone can tell) is still lurking in his victim's room. Well, let our name be vengeance. Call Bradshaw."

The footman came at the summons, very white and nervous.

"Put yourself together, Bradshaw," said the

lawyer. "This suspense, I know, is telling upon all of you; but it is now our intention to make an end of it. Poole, here, and I are going to force our way into the cabinet. If all is well, my shoulders are broad enough to bear the blame. Meanwhile, lest anything should really be amiss, or any malefactor seek to escape by the back, you and the boy must go round the corner with a pair of good sticks and take your post at the laboratory door. We give you ten minutes, to get to your stations."

As Bradshaw left, the lawyer looked at his watch. "And now, Poole, let us get to ours," he said; and taking the poker under his arm, led the way into the yard. The scud had banked over the moon, and it was now quite dark. The wind, which only broke in puffs and draughts into that deep well of building, tossed the light of the candle to and fro about their steps, until they came into the shelter of the theatre, where they sat down silently to wait. London hummed solemnly all around; but nearer at hand, the stillness was only broken by the sounds of a footfall moving to and fro along the cabinet floor.

"So it will walk all day, sir," whispered Poole; "ay, and the better part of the night. Only when a new sample comes from the chemist, there's a bit of a break. Ah, it's an ill conscience that's such an enemy to rest! Ah, sir, there's blood foully shed in every step of it! But hark again, a little closer—put your heart in your ears, Mr. Utterson, and tell me, is that the doctor's foot?"

The steps fell lightly and oddly, with a certain swing, for all they went so slowly; it was different indeed from the heavy creaking tread of Henry Jekyll. Utterson sighed. "Is there never anything else?" he asked.

Poole nodded. "Once," he said. "Once I heard it weeping!"

"Weeping? how that?" said the lawyer, conscious of a sudden chill of horror.

"Weeping like a woman or a lost soul," said the butler. "I came away with that upon my heart, that I could have wept too."

But now the ten minutes drew to an end. Poole disinterred the axe from under a stack of packing straw; the candle was set upon the nearest table to light them to the attack; and they drew near with bated breath to where that patient foot was still going up and down, up and down, in the quiet of the night. "Jekyll," cried Utterson, with a loud voice, "I demand to see you." He paused a moment, but there came no reply. "I give you fair warning, our suspicions are aroused, and I must and shall see you," he resumed; "if not by fair means, then by foul—if not of your consent, then by brute force!"

"Utterson," said the voice, "for God's sake, have mercy!"

"Ah, that's not Jekyll's voice—it's Hyde's!" cried Utterson. "Down with the door, Poole!"

Poole swung the axe over his shoulder; the blow shook the building, and the red baize door leaped against the lock and hinges. A dismal screech, as of mere animal terror, rang from the cabinet. Up went the axe again, and again the panels crashed and the frame bounded; four times the blow fell; but the wood was tough and the fittings were of excellent workmanship; and it was not until the fifth, that the lock burst and the wreck of the door fell inwards on the carpet.

The besiegers, appalled by their own riot and the stillness that had succeeded, stood back a little and peered in. There lay the cabinet before their eyes in the quiet lamplight, a good fire glowing and chattering on the hearth, the kettle singing its thin strain, a drawer or two open, papers neatly set forth on the business table, and nearer the fire, the things laid out for tea; the quietest room, you would have said, and, but for the glazed presses full of chemicals, the most commonplace that night in London.

Right in the midst there lay the body of a man sorely contorted and still twitching. They drew near on tiptoe, turned it on its back and beheld the face of Edward Hyde. He was dressed in clothes far too large for him, clothes of the doctor's bigness; the cords of his face still moved with a semblance of life, but life was quite gone: and by the crushed phial in the hand and the strong smell of kernels that hung upon the air, Utterson knew that he was looking on the body of a self-destroyer.

"We have come too late," he said sternly, "whether to save or punish. Hyde is gone to his account; and it only remains for us to find the body of your master."

The far greater proportion of the building was occupied by the theatre, which filled almost the whole ground storey and was lighted from above, and by the cabinet, which formed an upper story at one end and looked upon the court. A corridor joined the theatre to the door on the by-street; and with this the cabinet communicated separately by a second flight of stairs. There were besides a few dark closets and a spacious cellar. All these they now thoroughly examined. Each closet needed but a glance, for all were empty, and all, by the dust that fell from their doors, had stood long unopened. The cellar, indeed, was filled with crazy lumber, mostly dating from the times of the surgeon who was Jekyll's predecessor; but even as they opened the door they were advertised of the uselessness of further search, by the fall of a perfect mat of cobweb which had for years sealed up the entrance. Nowhere was there any trace of Henry Jekyll, dead or alive.

Poole stamped on the flags of the corridor. "He must be buried here," he said, hearkening to the sound.

"Or he may have fled," said Utterson, and he turned to examine the door in the by-street. It was locked; and lying near by on the flags, they found the key, already stained with rust.

"This does not look like use," observed the lawyer.

"Use!" echoed Poole. "Do you not see, sir, it is broken? much as if a man had stamped on it."

"Ay," continued Utterson, "and the fractures, too, are rusty." The two men looked at each other with a scare. "This is beyond me, Poole," said the lawyer. "Let us go back to the cabinet."

They mounted the stair in silence, and still with an occasional awestruck glance at the dead body, proceeded more thoroughly to examine the contents of the cabinet. At one table, there were traces of chemical work, various measured heaps of some white salt being laid on glass saucers, as though for an experiment in which the unhappy man had been prevented.

"That is the same drug that I was always bringing him," said Poole; and even as he spoke, the kettle with a startling noise boiled over.

This brought them to the fireside, where the

easychair was drawn cosily up, and the tea things stood ready to the sitter's elbow, the very sugar in the cup. There were several books on a shelf; one lay beside the tea things open, and Utterson was amazed to find it a copy of a pious work, for which Jekyll had several times expressed a great esteem, annotated, in his own hand, with startling blasphemies.

Next, in the course of their review of the chamber, the searchers came to the cheval-glass, into whose depths they looked with an involuntary horror. But it was so turned as to show them nothing but the rosy glow playing on the roof, the fire sparkling in a hundred repetitions along the glazed front of the presses, and their own pale and fearful countenances stooping to look in.

"This glass has seen some strange things, sir," whispered Poole.

"And surely none stranger than itself," echoed the lawyer in the same tones. "For what did Jekyll"—he caught himself up at the word with a start, and then conquering the weakness—"what could Jekyll want with it?" he said.

"You may say that!" said Poole.

Next they turned to the business table. On the desk, among the neat array of papers, a large envelope was uppermost, and bore, in the doctor's hand, the name of Mr. Utterson. The lawyer unsealed it, and several enclosures fell to the floor. The first was a will, drawn in the same eccentric terms as the one which he had returned six months before, to serve as a testament in case of death and as a deed of gift in case of disappearance; but in place of the name of Edward Hyde, the lawyer, with indescribable amazement, read the name of Gabriel John Utterson. He looked at Poole, and then back at the paper, and last of all at the dead malefactor stretched upon the carpet.

"My head goes round," he said. "He has been all these days in possession; he had no cause to like me; he must have raged to see himself displaced; and he has not destroyed this document."

He caught up the next paper; it was a brief note in the doctor's hand and dated at the top. "O Poole!" the lawyer cried, "he was alive and here this day. He cannot have been disposed of in so short a space; he must be still alive, he must have fled! And then, why fled? and how? and in that case, can we venture to declare this suicide? O, we must be careful. I foresee that we may yet involve your master in some dire catastrophe."

"Why don't you read it, sir?" asked Poole.

"Because I fear," replied the lawyer solemnly. "God grant I have no cause for it!" And with that he brought the paper to his eyes and read as follows:

My dear Utterson,—When this shall fall into your hands, I shall have disappeared, under what circumstances I have not the penetration to foresee, but my instinct and all the circumstances of my nameless situation tell me that the end is sure and must be early. Go then, and first read the narrative which Lanyon warned me he was to place in your hands; and if you care to hear more, turn to the confession of

Your unworthy and unhappy friend,

HENRY JEKYLL.

"There was a third enclosure?" asked Utterson.

"Here, sir," said Poole, and gave into his hands a considerable packet sealed in several places.

The lawyer put it in his pocket. "I would say nothing of this paper. If your master has fled or is dead, we may at least save his credit. It is now ten; I must go home and read these documents in quiet; but I shall be back before midnight, when we shall send for the police."

They went out, locking the door of the theatre behind them; and Utterson, once more leaving the servants gathered about the fire in the hall, trudged back to his office to read the two narratives in which this mystery was now to be explained.

DR. LANYON'S
NARRATIVE

On the ninth of January, now four days ago, I received by the evening delivery a registered envelope, addressed in the hand of my colleague and old school companion, Henry Jekyll. I was a good deal surprised by this; for we were by no means in the habit of correspondence; I had seen the man, dined with him, indeed, the night before; and I could imagine nothing in our intercourse that should justify formality of registration. The contents increased my wonder; for this is how the letter ran:

10th December, 18—.

Dear Lanyon,—You are one of my oldest friends; and although we may have differed at times on scientific questions, I cannot remember, at least on my side, any break in our affection. There was never a day when, if you had said to me, "Jekyll, my life, my honour, my reason, depend upon you," I would not have sacrificed my left hand to help you. Lanyon, my life, my honour, my reason, are all at your mercy; if you fail me to-night, I am lost. You might suppose, after this preface, that I am going to ask you for something dishonourable to grant. Judge for yourself.

I want you to postpone all other engagements for to-night—ay, even if you were summoned to the bedside of an emperor; to take a cab, unless your carriage should be actually at the door; and with this letter in your hand for consultation, to drive straight to my house. Poole, my butler, has his orders; you will find him waiting your arrival with a locksmith. The door of my cabinet is then to be forced: and you are to go in alone; to open the glazed press (letter E) on the left hand, breaking the lock if it be shut; and to draw out, *with all its contents as they stand,* the fourth drawer from the top or (which is the same thing) the third from the bottom. In my extreme distress of mind, I have a morbid fear of misdirecting you; but even if I am in error, you may know the right drawer by its contents: some powders, a phial and a paper book. This drawer I beg of you to carry back with you to Cavendish Square exactly as it stands.

That is the first part of the service: now for the second. You should be back, if you set out at once on the receipt of this, long before midnight; but I will leave you that amount of margin, not only in the fear of one of those obstacles that can neither be prevented nor foreseen, but because an hour when your servants are in bed is to be preferred for what will then remain to do. At midnight, then, I have to ask you to be alone in your consulting room, to admit with your own hand into the house a man who will present himself in my name, and to place in his hands the drawer that you will have brought with you from my cabinet. Then you will have played your part and earned my gratitude completely. Five minutes afterwards, if you insist upon an explanation, you will have understood that these arrangements are of capital importance; and that by the neglect of one of them, fantastic as they must appear, you might have charged your conscience with my death or the shipwreck of my reason.

Confident as I am that you will not trifle with this appeal, my heart sinks and my hand trembles at the bare thought of such a possibility. Think of me at this hour, in a strange place, labouring under a blackness of distress that no fancy can exaggerate, and yet well aware that, if you will but punctually serve me, my troubles will roll away like a story that is told. Serve me, my dear Lanyon, and save

Your friend,

H. J.

P.S.—I had already sealed this up when a fresh terror struck upon my soul. It is possible that the post-office may fail me, and this letter not come into your hands until to-morrow morning. In that case, dear Lanyon, do my errand when it shall be most convenient for you in the course of the day; and once more expect my messenger at midnight. It may then already be too late; and if that night passes without event, you will know that you have seen the last of Henry Jekyll.

Upon the reading of this letter, I made sure my colleague was insane; but till that was proved beyond the possibility of doubt, I felt bound to do as he requested. The less I understood of this farrago, the less I was in a position to judge of its importance; and an appeal so worded could not be set aside without a grave responsibility. I rose accordingly from table, got into a hansom, and drove straight to Jekyll's house. The butler was awaiting my arrival; he had received by the same post as mine a registered letter of instruction, and had sent at once for a locksmith and a carpenter. The tradesmen came while we were yet speaking; and we moved in a body to old Dr. Denman's surgical theatre, from which (as you are doubtless aware) Jekyll's private cabinet is most conveniently entered. The door was very strong, the lock excellent; the carpenter avowed he would have great trouble and have to do much damage, if force were to be used; and the locksmith was near despair. But this last was a handy fellow, and after two hours' work, the door stood open. The press marked E was unlocked; and I took out the drawer, had it filled up with straw and tied in a sheet, and returned with it to Cavendish Square.

Here I proceeded to examine its contents. The powders were neatly enough made up, but not with the nicety of the dispensing chemist; so that it was plain they were of Jekyll's private manufacture: and when I opened one of the wrappers I found what seemed to me a simple crystalline salt of a white colour. The phial, to which I next turned my attention, might have been about half full of a blood-red liquor, which was highly pungent to the sense of smell and seemed to me to contain phosphorus and some volatile ether. At the other ingredients I could make no guess. The book was an ordinary version book and contained little but a series of dates. These covered a period of many years, but I observed that the entries ceased nearly a year ago and quite abruptly. Here and there a brief remark was appended to a date, usually no more than a single word: "double" occurring perhaps six times in a total of several hundred entries; and once very early in the list and followed by several marks of exclamation, "total failure!!!" All this, though it whetted my curiosity, told me little that was definite. Here were a phial of some salt, and the record of a series of experiments that had led (like too many of Jekyll's investigations) to no end of practical usefulness. How could the presence of these articles in my house affect either the honour, the sanity, or the life of my flighty colleague? If his messenger could go to one place, why could he not go to another? And even granting some impediment, why was this gentleman to be received by me in secret? The more I reflected the more convinced I grew that I was dealing with a case of cerebral disease; and though I dismissed my servants to bed, I loaded an old revolver, that I might be found in some posture of self-defence.

Twelve o'clock had scarce rung out over London, ere the knocker sounded very gently on the door. I went myself at the summons, and found a small man crouching against the pillars of the portico.

"Are you come from Dr. Jekyll?" I asked.

He told me "yes" by a constrained gesture; and when I had bidden him enter, he did not obey me without a searching backward glance into the darkness of the square. There was a policeman not far off, advancing with his bull's eye open; and at the sight, I thought my visitor started and made greater haste.

These particulars struck me, I confess, disagreeably; and as I followed him into the bright light of the consulting room, I kept my hand ready on my weapon. Here, at last, I had a chance of clearly seeing him. I had never set eyes on him before, so much was certain. He was small, as I have said; I was struck besides with the shocking expression of his face, with his remarkable combination of great muscular activity and great apparent debility of constitution, and—last but not least—with the odd, subjective disturbance caused by his neighbourhood. This bore some resemblance to incipient rigour, and was accompanied by a marked sinking of the pulse. At the time, I set it down to some idiosyncratic, personal distaste, and merely wondered at the acuteness of the symptoms; but I have since had reason to believe the cause to lie much deeper in the nature of man, and to turn on some nobler hinge than the principle of hatred.

This person (who had thus, from the first

moment of his entrance, struck in me what I can only describe as a disgustful curiosity) was dressed in a fashion that would have made an ordinary person laughable; his clothes, that is to say, although they were of rich and sober fabric, were enormously too large for him in every measurement—the trousers hanging on his legs and rolled up to keep them from the ground, the waist of the coat below his haunches, and the collar sprawling wide upon his shoulders. Strange to relate, this ludicrous accoutrement was far from moving me to laughter. Rather, as there was something abnormal and misbegotten in the very essence of the creature that now faced me—something seizing, surprising and revolting—this fresh disparity seemed but to fit in with and to reinforce it; so that to my interest in the man's nature and character, there was added a curiosity as to his origin, his life, his fortune and status in the world.

These observations, though they have taken so great a space to be set down in, were yet the work of a few seconds. My visitor was, indeed, on fire with sombre excitement.

"Have you got it?" he cried. "Have you got it?" And so lively was his impatience that he even laid his hand upon my arm and sought to shake me.

I put him back, conscious at his touch of a certain icy pang along my blood. "Come, sir," said I. "You forget that I have not yet the pleasure of your acquaintance. Be seated, if you please." And I showed him an example, and sat down myself in my customary seat and with as fair an imitation of my ordinary manner to a patient, as the lateness of the hour, the nature of my preoccupations, and the horror I had of my visitor, would suffer me to muster.

"I beg your pardon, Dr. Lanyon," he replied civilly enough. "What you say is very well founded; and my impatience has shown its heels to my politeness. I come here at the instance of your colleague, Dr. Henry Jekyll, on a piece of business of some moment; and I understood . . ." He paused and put his hand to his throat, and I could see, in spite of his collected manner, that he was wrestling against the approaches of the hysteria—"I understood, a drawer . . ."

But here I took pity on my visitor's suspense, and some perhaps on my own growing curiosity.

"There it is, sir," said I, pointing to the drawer, where it lay on the floor behind a table and still covered with the sheet,

He sprang to it, and then paused, and laid his hand upon his heart: I could hear his teeth grate with the convulsive action of his jaws; and his face was so ghastly to see that I grew alarmed both for his life and reason.

"Compose yourself," said I.

He turned a dreadful smile to me, and as if with the decision of despair, plucked away the sheet. At sight of the contents, he uttered one loud sob of such immense relief that I sat petrified. And the next moment, in a voice that was already fairly well under control, "Have you a graduated glass?" he asked.

I rose from my place with something of an effort and gave him what he asked.

He thanked me with a smiling nod, measured out a few minims of the red tincture and added one of the powders. The mixture, which was at first a reddish hue, began, in proportion as the crystals melted to brighten in colour, to effervesce audibly, and to throw off small fumes of vapour. Suddenly and at the same moment, the ebullition ceased and the compound changed to a dark purple, which faded again more slowly to a watery green. My visitor, who had watched these metamorphoses with a keen eye, smiled, set down the glass upon the table, and then turned and looked upon me with an air of scrutiny.

"And now," said he, "to settle what remains. Will you be wise? will you be guided? will you suffer me to take this glass in my hand and to go forth from your house without further parley? or has the greed of curiosity too much command of you? Think before you answer, for it shall be done as you decide. As you decide, you shall be left as you were before, and neither richer nor wiser, unless the sense of service rendered to a man in mortal distress may be counted as a kind of riches of the soul. Or, if you shall so prefer to choose, a new province of knowledge and new avenues to fame and power shall be laid open to you, here, in this room, upon the instant; and your sight shall be blasted by a prodigy to stagger the unbelief of Satan."

"Sir," said I, affecting a coolness that I was far from truly possessing, "you speak enigmas, and you will perhaps not wonder that I hear you with no very strong impression of belief. But I have gone too far in the way of inexplicable services to pause before I see the end."

"It is well," replied my visitor. "Lanyon, you remember your vows: what follows is under the seal of our profession. And now, you who have so long been bound to the most narrow and material views, you who have denied the virtue of transcendental medicine, you who have derided your superiors—behold!"

He put the glass to his lips and drank at one gulp. A cry followed; he reeled, staggered, clutched at the table and held on, staring with injected eyes, gasping with open mouth; and as I looked there came, I thought, a change—he seemed to swell—his face became suddenly black and the features seemed to melt and alter—and the next moment, I had sprung to my feet and leaped back against the wall, my arm raised to shield me from that prodigy, my mind submerged in terror.

"O God!" I screamed, and "O God!" again and again; for there before my eyes—pale and shaken, and half fainting, and groping before him with his hands, like a man restored from death—there stood Henry Jekyll!

What he told me in the next hour, I cannot bring my mind to set on paper. I saw what I saw, I heard what I heard, and my soul sickened at it; and yet now when that sight has faded from my eyes, I ask myself if I believe it, and I cannot answer. My life is shaken to its roots; sleep has left me; the deadliest terror sits by me at all hours of the day and night; and I feel that my days are numbered, and that I must die; and yet I shall die incredulous. As for the moral turpitude that man unveiled to me, even with tears of penitence, I cannot, even in memory, dwell on it without a start of horror. I will say but one thing, Utterson, and that (if you can bring your mind to credit it) will be more than enough. The creature who crept into my house that night was, on Jekyll's own confession, known by the name of Hyde and hunted for in every corner of the land as the murderer of Carew.

HASTIE LANYON

HENRY JEKYLL'S
FULL STATEMENT
OF THE CASE

I was born in the year 18— to a large fortune, endowed besides with excellent parts, inclined by nature to industry, fond of the respect of the wise and good among my fellowmen, and thus, as might have been supposed, with every guarantee of an honourable and distinguished future. And indeed the worst of my faults was a certain impatient gaiety of disposition, such as has made the happiness of many, but such as I found it hard to reconcile with my imperious desire to carry my head high, and wear a more than commonly grave countenance before the public. Hence it came about that I concealed my pleasures; and that when I reached years of reflection, and began to look round me and take stock of my progress and position in the world, I stood already committed to a profound duplicity of life. Many a man would have even blazoned such irregularities as I was guilty of; but from the high views that I had set before me, I regarded and hid them with an almost morbid sense of shame. It was thus rather the exacting nature of my aspirations than any particular degradation in my faults, that made me what I was, and, with even a deeper trench than in the majority of men, severed in me those provinces of good and ill which divide and compound man's dual nature. In this case, I was driven to reflect deeply and inveterately on that hard law of life, which lies at the root of religion and is one of the most plentiful springs of distress. Though so profound a double-dealer, I was in no sense a hypocrite; both sides of me were in dead earnest; I was no more myself when I laid aside restraint and plunged in shame, than when I laboured, in the eye of day, at the furtherance of knowledge or the relief of sorrow and suffering. And it chanced that the direction of my scientific studies, which led wholly towards the mystic and the transcendental, reacted and shed a strong light on this consciousness of the perennial war among my members. With every day, and from both sides of my intelligence, the moral and the intellectual, I thus drew steadily nearer to that truth, by whose partial discovery I have been doomed to such a dreadful shipwreck: that man is not truly one, but truly two. I say two, because

the state of my own knowledge does not pass
beyond that point. Others will follow, others will
outstrip me on the same lines; and I hazard the
guess that man will be ultimately known for
a mere polity of multifarious, incongruous and
independent denizens. I, for my part, from the
nature of my life, advanced infallibly in one
direction and in one direction only. It was on the
moral side, and in my own person, that I learned
to recognise the thorough and primitive duality of
man; I saw that, of the two natures that
contended in the field of my consciousness, even
if I could rightly be said to be either, it was only
because I was radically both; and from an early
date, even before the course of my scientific
discoveries had begun to suggest the most naked
possibility of such a miracle, I had learned to
dwell with pleasure, as a beloved daydream, on
the thought of the separation of these elements. If
each, I told myself, could be housed in separate
identities, life would be relieved of all that was
unbearable; the unjust might go his way, de-
livered from the aspirations and remorse of his
more upright twin; and the just could walk
steadfastly and securely on his upward path,
doing the good things in which he found his
pleasure, and no longer exposed to disgrace and
penitence by the hands of this extraneous evil. It
was the curse of mankind that these incongruous

faggots were thus bound together—that in the agonised womb of consciousness, these polar twins should be continuously struggling. How, then, were they dissociated?

I was so far in my reflections when, as I have said, a side light began to shine upon the subject from the laboratory table. I began to perceive more deeply than it has ever yet been stated, the trembling immateriality, the mistlike transience, of this seemingly so solid body in which we walk attired. Certain agents I found to have the power to shake and pluck back that fleshly vestment, even as a wind might toss the curtains of a pavilion. For two good reasons, I will not enter deeply into this scientific branch of my confession. First, because I have been made to learn that the doom and burthen of our life is bound for ever on man's shoulders, and when the attempt is made to cast it off, it but returns upon us with more unfamiliar and more awful pressure. Second, because, as my narrative will make, alas! too evident, my discoveries were incomplete. Enough then, that I not only recognised my natural body from the mere aura and effulgence of certain of the powers that made up my spirit, but managed to compound a drug by which these powers should be dethroned from their supremacy, and a second form and countenance substituted, none the less natural to me because they were the expression, and bore the stamp of lower elements in my soul.

I hesitated long before I put this theory to the test of practice. I knew well that I risked death; for any drug that so potently controlled and shook the very fortress of identity, might, by the least scruple of an overdose or at the least inopportunity in the moment of exhibition, utterly blot out that immaterial tabernacle which I looked to it to change. But the temptation of a discovery so singular and profound at last overcame the suggestions of alarm. I had long since prepared my tincture; I purchased at once, from a firm of wholesale chemists, a large quantity of a particular salt which I knew, from my experiments, to be the last ingredient required; and late one accursed night, I compounded the elements, watched them boil and smoke together in the glass, and when the ebullition had subsided, with a strong glow of courage, drank off the potion.

The most racking pangs succeeded: a grinding in the bones, deadly nausea, and a horror of the spirit that cannot be exceeded at the hour of birth or death. Then these agonies began swiftly to subside, and I came to myself as if out of a great sickness. There was something strange in my sensations, something indescribably new and, from its very novelty, incredibly sweet. I felt younger, lighter, happier in body; within I was conscious of a heady recklessness, a current of disordered sensual images running like a millrace in my fancy, a solution of the bonds of obligation, an unknown but not an innocent freedom of the soul. I knew myself, at the first breath of this new life, to be more wicked, tenfold more wicked, sold a slave to my original evil; and the thought, in that moment, braced and delighted me like wine. I stretched out my hands, exulting in the freshness of these sensations; and in the act, I was suddenly aware that I had lost in stature.

There was no mirror, at that date, in my room; that which stands beside me as I write, was brought there later on and for the very purpose of these transformations. The night, however, was far gone into the morning—the morning, black as it was, was nearly ripe for the conception of the day—the inmates of my house were locked in the most rigorous hours of slumber; and I determined, flushed as I was with hope and triumph, to venture in my new shape as far as to my bedroom. I crossed the yard, wherein the constellations looked down upon me, I could have thought, with wonder, the first creature of that sort that their unsleeping vigilance had yet disclosed to them; I stole through the corridors, a stranger in my own house; and coming to my room, I saw for the first time the appearance of Edward Hyde.

I must here speak by theory alone, saying not that which I know, but which I suppose to be most probable. The evil side of my nature, to which I had now transferred the stamping efficacy, was less robust and less developed than the good which I had just deposed. Again, in the course of my life, which had been, after all, nine tenths a life of effort, virtue and control, it had been much less exercised and much less exhausted. And hence, as I think, it came about that Edward Hyde was so much smaller, slighter and younger than Henry Jekyll. Even as good shone upon the countenance of the one, evil was written broadly and plainly on the face of the other. Evil besides (which I must still believe to be the lethal side of man) had left on that body and imprint of deformity and decay. And yet when I looked upon that ugly idol in the glass, I was conscious of no repugnance, rather of a leap of welcome. This, too, was myself. It seemed natural and human. In my eyes it bore a livelier image of the spirit, it seemed more express and single, than the imperfect and divided countenance I had been hitherto accustomed to call mine. And in so far I was doubtless right. I have observed that when I wore the semblance of Edward Hyde, none could come near to me at first without a visible misgiving of the flesh. This, as I take it, was because all human beings, as we meet them, are commingled out of good and evil: and Edward Hyde, alone in the ranks of mankind, was pure evil.

I lingered but a moment at the mirror: the second and conclusive experiment had yet to be attempted; it yet remained to be seen if I had lost my identity beyond redemption and must flee before daylight from a house that was no longer mine; and hurrying back to my cabinet, I once more prepared and drank the cup, once more suffered the pangs of dissolution, and came to myself once more with the character, the stature and the face of Henry Jekyll.

That night I had come to the fatal cross-roads. Had I approached my discovery in a more noble spirit, had I risked the experiment while under the empire of generous or pious aspirations, all must have been otherwise, and from these agonies of death and birth, I had come forth an angel instead of a fiend. The drug had no discriminating action; it was neither diabolical nor divine; it but shook the doors of the prisonhouse of my disposition; and like the captives of Philippi, that which stood within ran forth. At that time my virtue slumbered; my evil, kept awake by ambition, was alert and swift to seize the occasion; and the thing that was projected was Edward Hyde. Hence, although I had now two characters as well as two appearances, one was wholly evil, and the other was still the old Henry Jekyll, that incongruous compound of whose reformation and improvement I had already learned to despair. The movement was thus wholly toward the worse.

Even at that time, I had not conquered my aversions to the dryness of a life of study. I would still be merrily disposed at times; and as my pleasures were (to say the least) undignified, and I was not only well known and highly considered, but growing towards the elderly man, this incoherency of my life was daily growing more unwelcome. It was on this side that my new power tempted me until I fell in slavery. I had but to drink the cup, to doff at once the body of the noted professor, and to assume, like a thick cloak, that of Edward Hyde. I smiled at the notion; it seemed to me at the time to be humourous; and I made my preparations with the most studious care. I took and furnished that house in Soho, to which Hyde was tracked by the police; and engaged as a housekeeper a creature whom I knew well to be silent and unscrupulous. On the other side, I announced to my servants that a Mr. Hyde (whom I described) was to have full liberty and power about my house in the square; and to parry mishaps, I even called and made myself a familiar object, in my second character. I next drew up that will to which you so much objected; so that if anything befell me in the person of Dr. Jekyll, I could enter on that of Edward Hyde without pecuniary loss. And thus fortified, as I supposed, on every side, I began to profit by the strange immunities of my position.

Men have before hired bravos to transact their crimes, while their own person and reputation sat under shelter. I was the first that ever did so for his pleasures. I was the first that could plod in the public eye with a load of genial respectability, and in a moment, like a schoolboy, strip off these lendings and spring headlong into the sea of liberty. But for me, in my impenetrable mantle, the safety was complete. Think of it—I did not even exist! Let me but escape into my laboratory door, give me but a second or two to mix and swallow the draught that I had always standing ready; and whatever he had done, Edward Hyde would pass away like the stain of breath upon a mirror; and there in his stead, quietly at home, trimming the midnight lamp in his study, a man who could afford to laugh at suspicion, would be Henry Jekyll.

The pleasures which I made haste to seek in my disguise were, as I have said, undignified; I would scarce use a harder term. But in the hands of Edward Hyde, they soon began to turn toward the monstrous. When I would come back from these excursions, I was often plunged into a kind of wonder at my vicarious depravity. This familiar that I called out of my own soul, and sent forth alone to do his good pleasure, was a being inherently malign and villainous; his every act and thought centered on self; drinking pleasure with bestial avidity from any degree of torture to another; relentless like a man of stone. Henry Jekyll stood at times aghast before the acts of Edward Hyde; but the situation was apart from ordinary laws, and insidiously relaxed the grasp of conscience. It was Hyde, after all, and Hyde alone, that was guilty. Jekyll was no worse; he woke again to his good qualities seemingly unimpaired; he would even make haste, where it was possible, to undo the evil done by Hyde. And thus his conscience slumbered.

Into the details of the infamy at which I thus connived (for even now I can scarce grant that I committed it) I have no design of entering; I mean but to point out the warnings and the successive steps with which my chastisement approached. I met with one accident which, as it brought on no consequence, I shall no more than mention. An act of cruelty to a child aroused against me the anger of a passer-by, whom I recognised the other day in the person of your kinsman; the doctor and the child's family joined him; there were moments when I feared for my life; and at last, in order to pacify their too just resentment, Edward Hyde had to bring them to the door, and pay them in a cheque drawn in the name of Henry Jekyll. But this danger was easily eliminated from the future, by opening an account at another bank in the name of Edward Hyde himself; and when, by sloping my own hand backward, I had supplied my double with a signature, I thought I sat beyond the reach of fate.

Some two months before the murder of Sir Danvers, I had been out for one of my adventures, had returned at a late hour, and woke the next day in bed with somewhat odd sensations. It was in vain I looked about me; in vain I saw the decent furniture and tall proportions of my room in the square; in vain that I recognised the pattern of the bed curtains and the design of the mahogany frame; something still kept insisting that I was not where I was, that I had not wakened where I seemed to be, but in the little room in Soho where I was accustomed to sleep in the body of Edward Hyde. I smiled to myself, and, in my psychological way, began lazily to inquire into the elements of this illusion, occasionally, even as I did so, dropping back into a comfortable morning doze. I was still so engaged when, in one of my more wakeful moments, my eyes fell upon my hand. Now the hand of Henry Jekyll (as you have often re-marked) was professional in shape and size: it was large, firm, white and comely. But the hand which I now saw, clearly enough, in the yellow light of a mid-London morning, lying half shut on the bedclothes, was lean, corded, knuckly, of a dusky pallor and thickly shaded with a swart growth of hair. It was the hand of Edward Hyde.

I must have stared upon it for near half a minute, sunk as I was in the mere stupidity of wonder, before terror woke up in my breast as sudden and startling as the crash of cymbals; and bounding from my bed, I rushed to the mirror. At the sight that met my eyes, my blood was changed into something exquisitely thin and icy. Yes, I had gone to bed Henry Jekyll, I had awakened Edward Hyde. How was this to be explained? I asked myself; and then, with another bound of terror—how was it to be remedied? It was well on in the morning; the servants were up; all my drugs were in the cabinet—a long journey down two pairs of stairs, through the back passage, across the open court and through the anatomical theatre, from where I was then standing horror-struck. It might indeed be possible to cover my face; but of what use was that, when I was unable to conceal the alteration of my stature? And then with an overpowering sweetness of relief, it came back upon my mind that the servants were already used to the coming and going of my second self. I had soon dressed, as well as I was able, in clothes of my own size: had soon passed through the house, where Bradshaw stared and drew back at seeing Mr. Hyde at such an hour and in such a strange array; and ten minutes later, Dr. Jekyll had returned to his own shape and was sitting down, with a darkened brow, to make a feint of breakfasting,

Small indeed was my appetite. This inexplicable incident, this reversal of my previous experience, seemed, like the Babylonian finger on the wall, to be spelling out the letters of my judgment; and I began to reflect more seriously than ever before on the issues and possibilities of my double existence. That part of me which I had the power of projecting, had lately been much exercised and nourished; it had seemed to me of late as though the body of Edward Hyde had grown in stature, as though (when I wore that form) I were conscious of a more generous tide of blood; and I began to spy a danger that, if this were much prolonged, the balance of my nature might be permanently overthrown, the power of voluntary change be forfeited, and the character of Edward Hyde become irrevocably mine. The power of the drug had not been always equally displayed. Once, very early in my career, it had totally failed me; since then I had been obliged on more than one occasion to double, and once, with infinite risk of death, to treble the amount; and these rare uncertainties had cast hitherto the sole shadow on my contentment. Now, however, and in the light of that morning's accident, I was led to remark that whereas, in the beginning, the difficulty had been to throw off the body of Jekyll, it had of late gradually but decidedly transferred itself to the other side. All things therefore seemed to point to this; that I was slowly losing hold of my original and better self, and becoming slowly incorporated with my second and worse.

Between these two, I now felt I had to choose. My two natures had memory in common, but all other faculties were most unequally shared between them. Jekyll (who was composite) now with the most sensitive apprehensions, now with a greedy gusto, projected and shared in the pleasures and adventures of Hyde; but Hyde was indifferent to Jekyll, or but remembered him as the mountain bandit remembers the cavern in which he conceals himself from pursuit. Jekyll had more than a father's interest; Hyde had more of a son's indifference. To cast in my lot with Jekyll, was to die to those appetites which I had long secretly indulged and had of late begun to pamper. To cast it in with Hyde, was to die to a thousand interests and aspirations, and to become, at a blow and forever, despised and friendless. The bargain might appear unequal; but there was still another consideration in the scales; for while Jekyll would suffer smartingly in the fires of abstinence, Hyde would be not even conscious of all that he had lost. Strange as my circumstances were, the terms of this debate are as old and commonplace as man; much the same inducements and alarms cast the die for any tempted and trembling sinner; and it fell out with me, as it falls with so vast a majority of my fellows, that I chose the better part and was found wanting in the strength to keep to it.

Yes, I preferred the elderly and discontented doctor, surrounded by friends and cherishing honest hopes; and bade a resolute farewell to the liberty, the comparative youth, the light step, leaping impulses and secret pleasures, that I had enjoyed in the disguise of Hyde. I made this choice perhaps with some unconscious reservation, for I neither gave up the house in Soho, nor destroyed the clothes of Edward Hyde, which still lay ready in my cabinet. For two months, however, I was true to my determination; for two months, I led a life of such severity as I had never before attained to, and enjoyed the compensations of an approving conscience. But time began at last to obliterate the freshness of my alarm; the praises of conscience began to grow into a thing of course; I began to be tortured with throes and longings, as of Hyde struggling for freedom; and at last, in an hour of moral weakness, I once again compounded and swallowed the transforming draught.

I do not suppose that, when a drunkard reasons with himself upon his vice, he is once out of five hundred times affected by the dangers that he runs through his brutish, physical insensibility; neither had I, long as I had considered my position, made enough allowance for the complete moral insensibility and insensate readiness to evil, which were the leading characters of Edward Hyde. Yet it was by these that I was punished. My devil had been long caged, he came out roaring. I was conscious, even when I took the draught, of a more unbridled, a more furious propensity to ill. It must have been this, I suppose, that stirred in my soul that tempest of impatience with which I listened to the civilities of my unhappy victim; I declare, at least, before God, no man morally sane could have been guilty of that crime upon so pitiful a provocation; and that I struck in no more reasonable spirit than that in which a sick child may break a plaything. But I had voluntarily stripped myself of all those balancing instincts by which even the worst of us continues to walk with some degree of steadiness among temptations; and in my case, to be tempted, however slightly, was to fall.

Instantly the spirit of hell awoke in me and raged. With a transport of glee, I mauled the unresisting body, tasting delight from every blow;

and it was not till weariness had begun to succeed, that I was suddenly, in the top fit of my delirium, struck through the heart by a cold thrill of terror. A mist dispersed; I saw my life to be forfeit; and fled from the scene of these excesses, at once glorying and trembling, my lust of evil gratified and stimulated, my love of life screwed to the topmost peg. I ran to the house in Soho, and (to make assurance doubly sure) destroyed my papers; thence I set out through the lamplit streets, in the same divided ecstasy of mind, gloating on my crime, light-headedly devising others in the future, and yet still hastening and still hearkening in my wake for the steps of the avenger. Hyde had a song upon his lips as he compounded the draught, and as he drank it, pledged the dead man. The pangs of trans-formation had not done tearing him, before Henry Jekyll, with streaming tears of gratitude and remorse, had fallen upon his knees and lifted his clasped hands to God. The veil of self-indulgence was rent from head to foot. I saw my life as a whole: I followed it up from the days of childhood, when I had walked with my father's hand, and through the self-denying toils of my professional life, to arrive again and again, with the same sense of unreality, at the damned horrors of the evening. I could have screamed aloud; I sought with tears and prayers to smother down the crowd of hideous images and sounds with which my memory swarmed against me; and still, between the petitions, the ugly face of my iniquity stared into my soul. As the acuteness of this remorse began to die away, it was succeeded by a sense of joy. The problem of my conduct was solved. Hyde was thenceforth impossible; whether I would or not, I was now confined to the better part of my existence; and O, how I rejoiced to think of it! with what willing humility I embraced anew the restrictions of natural life! with what sincere renunciation I locked the door by which I had so often gone and come, and ground the key under my heel!

The next day, came the news that the murder had been overlooked, that the guilt of Hyde was patent to the world, and that the victim was a man high in public estimation. It was not only a crime, it had been a tragic folly. I think I was glad to know it; I think I was glad to have my better impulses thus buttressed and guarded by the terrors of the scaffold. Jekyll was now my city of refuge; let but Hyde peep out an instant, and the hands of all men would be raised to take and slay him.

I resolved in my future conduct to redeem the past; and I can say with honesty that my resolve was fruitful of some good. You know yourself how earnestly, in the last months of the last year,

I laboured to relieve suffering; you know that much was done for others, and that the days passed quietly, almost happily for myself. Nor can I truly say that I wearied of this beneficent and innocent life; I think instead that I daily enjoyed it more completely; but I was still cursed with my duality of purpose; and as the first edge of my penitence wore off, the lower side of me, so long indulged, so recently chained down, began to growl for licence. Not that I dreamed of resuscitating Hyde; the bare idea of that would startle me to frenzy: no, it was in my own person that I was once more tempted to trifle with my conscience; and it was as an ordinary secret sinner that I at last fell before the assaults of temptation.

There comes an end to all things; the most capacious measure is filled at last; and this brief condescension to my evil finally destroyed the balance of my soul. And yet I was not alarmed; the fall seemed natural, like a return to the old days before I had made my discovery. It was a fine, clear, January day, wet under foot where the frost had melted, but cloudless overhead; and the Regent's Park was full of winter chirrupings and sweet with spring odours. I sat in the sun on a bench; the animal within me licking the chops of memory; the spiritual side a little drowsed, promising subsequent penitence, but not yet moved to begin. After all, I reflected, I was like my neighbours; and then I smiled, comparing myself with other men, comparing my active good-will with the lazy cruelty of their neglect. And at the very moment of that vainglorious thought, a qualm came over me, a horrid nausea and the most deadly shuddering. These passed away, and left me faint; and then as in its turn faintness subsided, I began to be aware of a change in the temper of my thoughts, a greater boldness, a contempt of danger, a solution of the bonds of obligation. I looked down; my clothes hung formlessly on my shrunken limbs; the hand that lay on my knee was corded and hairy. I was once more Edward Hyde. A moment before I had been safe of all men's respect, wealthy, beloved— the cloth laying for me in the dining-room at home; and now I was the common quarry of mankind, hunted, houseless, a known murderer, thrall to the gallows.

My reason wavered, but it did not fail me utterly. I have more than once observed that, in my second character, my faculties seemed sharpened to a point and my spirits more tensely elastic; thus it came about that, where Jekyll perhaps might have succumbed, Hyde rose to the importance of the moment. My drugs were in one of the presses of my cabinet; how was I to reach them? That was the problem that (crushing my temples in my hands) I set myself to solve. The laboratory door I had closed. If I sought to enter by the house, my own servants would consign me to the gallows. I saw I must employ another hand, and thought of Lanyon. How was he to be reached? how persuaded? Supposing that I escaped capture in the streets, how was I to make my way into his presence? and how should I, an unknown and displeasing visitor, prevail on the famous physician to rifle the study of his colleague, Dr. Jekyll? Then I remembered that of my original character, one part remained to me: I could write my own hand; and once I had conceived that kindling spark, the way that I must follow became lighted up from end to end.

Thereupon, I arranged my clothes as best I could, and summoning a passing hansom, drove to an hotel in Portland Street, the name of which I chanced to remember. At my appearance (which was indeed comical enough, however tragic a fate these garments covered) the driver could not conceal his mirth. I gnashed my teeth upon him with a gust of devilish fury; and the smile withered from his face—happily for him—yet more happily for myself, for in another instant I had certainly dragged him from his perch. At the inn, as I entered, I looked about me with so black a countenance as made the attendants tremble; not a look did they exchange in my presence; but obsequiously took my orders, led me to a private room, and brought me wherewithal to write. Hyde in danger of his life was a creature new to me; shaken with inordinate anger, strung to the pitch of murder, lusting to inflict pain. Yet the creature was astute; mastered his fury with a great effort of the will; composed two important letters, one to Lanyon and one to Poole; and that he might receive actual evidence of their being posted, sent them out with directions that they should be registered. Thenceforward, he sat all day over the fire in the private room, gnawing his nails; there he dined, sitting alone with his fears, the waiter visibly quailing before his eye; and thence, when the night was fully come, he set forth in the corner of a closed cab, and was driven to and fro about the streets of the city. He, I say—I cannot say, I. That child of Hell had nothing human; nothing lived in him but fear and hatred. And when at last, thinking the driver had begun to grow suspicious, he discharged the cab and ventured on foot, attired in his misfitting clothes, an object marked out for observation, into the midst of the nocturnal passengers, these two base passions raged within him like a tempest. He walked fast, hunted by his fears, chattering to himself, skulking through the less frequented thoroughfares, counting the minutes that still divided him from midnight. Once a woman spoke to him, offering, I think, a box of lights. He smote her in the face, and she fled.

When I came to myself at Lanyon's, the horror of my old friend perhaps affected me somewhat: I do not know; it was at least but a drop in the sea to the abhorrence with which I looked back upon these hours. A change had come over me. It was no longer the fear of the gallows, it was the horror of being Hyde that racked me. I received Lanyon's condemnation partly in a dream; it was partly in a dream that I came home to my own house and got into bed. I slept after the prostration of the day, with a stringent and profound slumber which not even the nightmares that wrung me could avail to break, I awoke in the morning shaken, weakened, but refreshed. I still hated and feared the thought of the brute that slept within me, and I had not of course forgotten the appalling dangers of the day before; but I was once more at home, in my own house and close to my drugs; and gratitude for my escape shone so strong in my soul that it almost rivalled the brightness of hope.

I was stepping leisurely across the court after breakfast, drinking the chill of the air with pleasure, when I was seized again with those indescribable sensations that heralded the change; and I had but the time to gain the shelter of my cabinet, before I was once again raging and freezing with the passions of Hyde. It took on this occasion a double dose to recall me to myself; and alas! six hours after, as I sat looking sadly in the fire, the pangs returned, and the drug had to be re-administered. In short, from that day forth it seemed only by a great effort as of gymnastics, and only under the immediate stimulation of the drug, that I was able to wear the countenance of Jekyll. At all hours of the day and night, I would be taken with the premonitory shudder; above all, if I slept, or even dozed for a moment in my chair, if was always as Hyde that I awakened. Under the strain of this continually impending doom and by the sleeplessness to which I now condemned myself, ay, even beyond what I had thought possible to man, I became, in my own person, a creature eaten up and emptied by fever, languidly weak both in body and mind, and solely occupied by one thought: the horror of my other self. But when I slept, or when the virtue of the medicine wore off, I would leap almost without transition (for the pangs of transformation grew daily less marked) into the possession of a fancy brimming with images of terror, a soul boiling with causeless hatreds, and a body that seemed not strong enough to contain the raging energies of life. The powers of Hyde seemed to have grown with the sickliness of Jekyll. And certainly the hate that now divided them was equal on each side. With Jekyll, it was a thing of vital instinct. He had now seen the full deformity of that creature that shared with him some of the phenomena of consciousness, and was co-heir with him to death: and beyond these links of community, which in themselves made the most poignant part of his distress, he thought of Hyde, for all his energy of life, as of something not only hellish but inorganic. This was the shocking thing; that the slime of the pit seemed to utter cries and voices; that the amorphous dust gesticulated and sinned; that what was dead, and had no shape, should usurp the offices of life. And this again, that that insurgent horror was knit to him closer than a wife, closer than an eye; lay caged in his flesh, where he heard it mutter and felt it struggle to be born; and at every hour of weakness, and in the confidence of slumber, prevailed against him, and deposed him out of life. The hatred of Hyde for Jekyll was of a different order. His terror of the gallows drove him continually to commit temporary suicide, and return to his subordinate station of a part instead of a person; but he loathed the necessity, he loathed the despondency into which Jekyll was now fallen, and he resented the dislike with which he was himself regarded. Hence the ape-like tricks that he would play me, scrawling in my own hand blasphemies on the pages of my books, burning the letters and destroying the portrait of my father; and indeed, had it not been for his fear of death, he would long ago have ruined himself in order to involve me in the ruin. But his love of life is wonderful; I go further: I, who sicken and freeze at the mere thought of him, when I recall the abjection and passion of this attachment, and when I know how he fears my power to cut him off by suicide, I find it in my heart to pity him.

It is useless, and the time awfully fails me, to prolong this description; no one has ever suffered such torments, let that suffice; and yet even to these, habit brought—no, not alleviation—but a certain callousness of soul, a certain acquiescence of despair; and my punishment might have gone on for years, but for the last calamity which has now fallen, and which has finally severed me from my own face and nature. My provision of the salt, which had never been renewed since the date of the first experiment, began to run low. I sent out for a fresh supply and mixed the draught; the ebullition followed, and the first change of colour, not the second; I drank it and it was without efficiency. You will learn from Poole how I have had London ransacked; it was in vain; and I am now persuaded that my first supply was impure, and that it was that unknown impurity which lent efficacy to the draught.

About a week has passed, and I am now finishing this statement under the influence of the last of the old powders. This, then, is the last time, short of a miracle, that Henry Jekyll can think his own thoughts or see his own face (now how sadly altered!) in the glass. Nor must I delay too long to bring my writing to an end; for if my narrative has hitherto escaped destruction, it has been by a combination of great prudence and great good luck. Should the throes of change take me in the act of writing it, Hyde will tear it in pieces; but if some time shall have elapsed after I have laid it by, his wonderful selfishness and circumscription to the moment will probably save it once again from the action of his ape-like spite. And indeed the doom that is closing on us both has already changed and crushed him. Half an hour from now, when I shall again and forever reindue that hated personality, I know how I shall sit shuddering and weeping in my chair, or continue, with the most strained and fearstruck ecstasy of listening, to pace up and down this room (my last earthly refuge) and give ear to every sound of menace. Will Hyde die upon the scaffold? or will he find courage to release himself at the last moment? God knows; I am careless; this is my true hour of death, and what is to follow concerns another than myself. Here then, as I lay down the pen and proceed to seal up my confession, I bring the life of that unhappy Henry Jekyll to an end.